ARESTANA
The Key Quest

Book I of the Arestana Series

Shawn P. B. Robinson

BrainSwell Publishing
Ingersoll, Ontario

ISBN 978-1-7751903-0-1

Interior Art by Allan Jensen

BrainSwell Publishing
Ingersoll, ON

Dedication and Thanks

To my wonderful wife who has tolerated my sense of humor along with my odd imagination. To my two sons, Liam and Ezra, after whom the two main characters are named. To all my editors and advisors who told me what I wanted to hear and who told me what I didn't want to hear: Rob, Hannah, Lydia, Hollie, Karlie, Mom (of the birth variety), Mom (of the in-law variety), Allan, Nate, Aunt Elizabeth and Luke.

All of you helped in some way in the editing or the publishing aspect of getting this book to print! For those I missed, please remember that I had encephalitis. I've forgotten much in this last year.

I would also like to give a special thanks to Suzanne Anderson (although I've never actually met her) as her book on Self-Publishing in Canada was especially helpful to me.

I would also like to dedicate this book to everyone, everywhere on this planet, named Peter P. Peterson.

Now, for those of you who like allegory or deeper meaning in books, please understand that this book is intended not to have deeper meaning or allegory. Feel free to search for it, but don't be disappointed if you come up with really insightful meanings for characters or experiences or places and in the end of the day… you're just wrong. ☺ Characters/places/etc. do not represent anything else (even in the book). It's a fun book.
Everything is fiction in this book.

Preface

The way this book came about was a bit of a surprise for me. I was doing well. I was exercising regularly, eating well and feeling great! And then I started to notice some problems.

Eight days after noticing some pain in my eye, I was lying in an isolation room in the hospital, vaguely aware of the fact that I could die from my diagnosis of encephalitis.

As I lay there, spending my time thinking, praying, wondering about life and death, I thought to myself that I would write a bedtime story for my two sons, Liam and Ezra. I used to tell them stories all the time before bed, and I thought it would be fun to type one up.

Perhaps it was because my brain wasn't quite right (encephalitis is a problem with the brain), but the story ended up being really weird. It also ended up being huge, and after I finished, I was encouraged by one of my first readers to publish it.

Since then, those who have read this book (children and adults alike) have either really loved the book or have been too uncomfortable to tell me it stinks. On top of that, two more books have grown out of this story and have turned this whole adventure into a series!

I hope you enjoy Arestana. It's been a blast for me to write and a joy for me to share!

Shawn P. B. Robinson
P.S. I expect you're wondering if my middle names are Peanut Butter. I can see why you would wonder that.

Books by Shawn P. B. Robinson

Available in Print or ebook

Jerry the Squirrel: Volume I
Arestana I: The Key Quest

Coming Soon

Arestana II: The Defense Quest	Coming Jun. 4, 2018
Arestana III: The Harry Quest	Coming Nov. 5, 2018
Jerry the Squirrel: Volume II	Coming, but who knows when. Keep your eye out!

www.shawnpbrobinson.com

www.amazon.com/author/shawnpbrobinson

www.facebook.com/shawnpbrobinsonauthor/

@shawnpbrobinson

Table of Contents

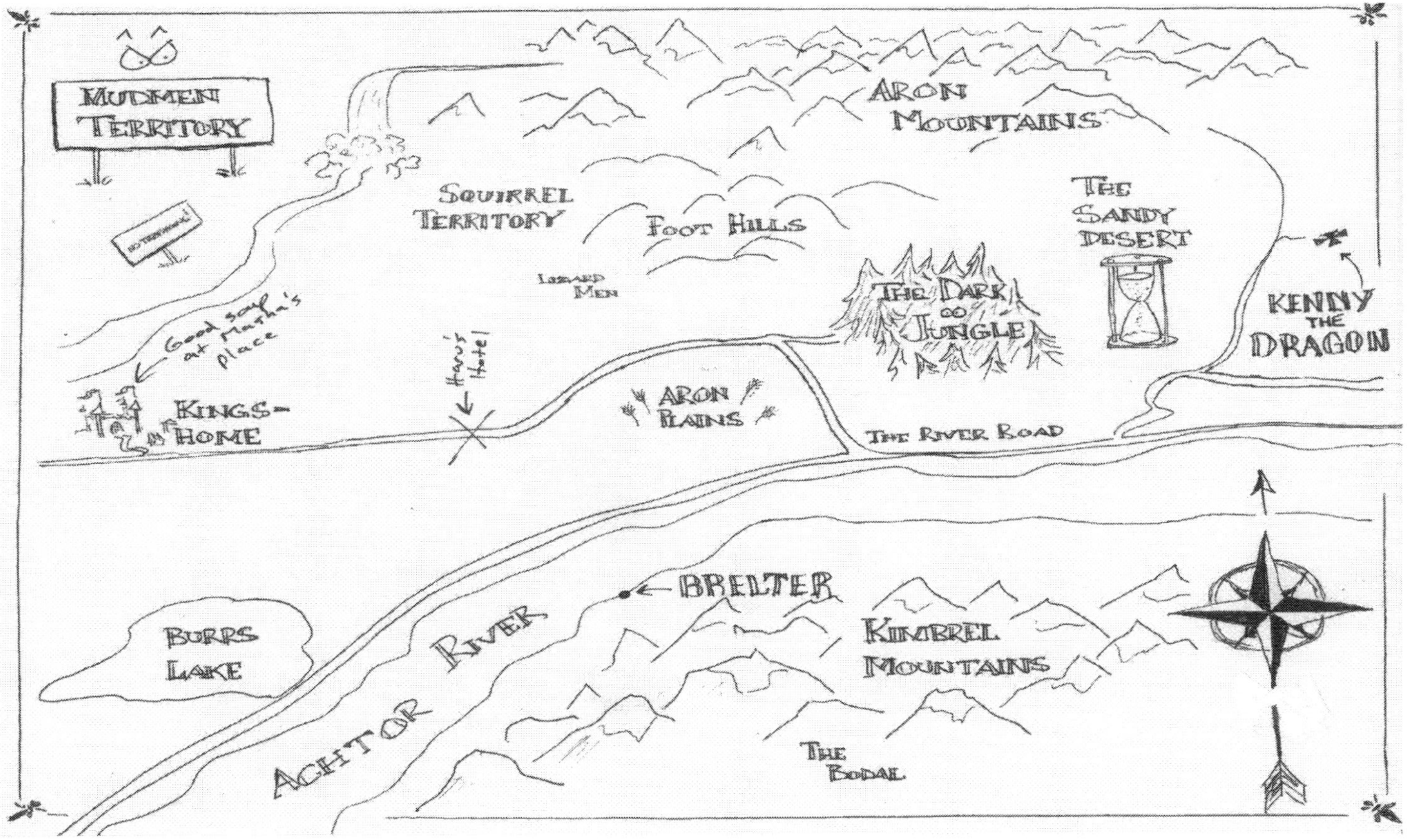
MUDMEN TERRITORY
ARON MOUNTAINS
SQUIRREL TERRITORY
FOOT HILLS
THE SANDY DESERT
LIZARD MEN
THE DARK JUNGLE
KENNY THE DRAGON
Good soup at Martha's place
Harv's Hotel
KINGS-HOME
ARON PLAINS
THE RIVER ROAD
BRELTER
BURRS LAKE
RIVER
ACHTOR
KIMBREL MOUNTAINS
THE BODAL

Prologue

Kenny growled. There was no one in sight who could hear it, but it felt good. He hoped maybe it was loud enough to echo down the corridors of the castle and catch the ear of some poor, easily frightened guard or kitchen worker. He liked to scare people, and he was good at it.

He would have come during the day. That was his original plan. He had planned to come when the castle was full of people and scare everyone all at once. When they saw him, they would have been terrified! He was a scary guy.

He had just run into a bit of a problem. That morning he had awakened with a terrible cold. The cold itself wasn't a problem. The cold lowered his voice which meant his growls were even scarier than normal. It was the way he sneezed. He was a bad sneezer. He couldn't do it in a scary way. The sound of each "achoo" came out as a short, soft, high pitched sneeze. The kind of sneeze you'd hear from a kitten and then say, "Ahhh... wasn't that adorable. Did you hear that sneeze? Maybe he'll do it again."

He wasn't going to rush into the middle of a crowded throne room, full of nobles and Knights and Lords and Ladies and roar, "Give me the key!" followed by a little kitten sneeze, "achoo!" He would never live it down. The only solution was to come by night. The castle was pretty much deserted.

His scale covered body moved through the quiet corridors. His feet made very little sound on the stone floor. The only noise was his long, scaly tail scraping quietly across the floor, interrupted by the occasional kitten sneeze.

He growled again as movement caught his eye up ahead. A guard walked around the corner with sword drawn and a fierce look on his face.

They stood before one another for a long time. Kenny stared down his opponent. His opponent didn't move.

The first one to speak was the guard. "Hark! Who goes there?"

Kenny thought it was pretty obvious. Kenny was big and hard to miss standing there in the corridor. Add to that the fact that there weren't many of his kind around. The guard should be able to see Kenny and know immediately who he was, but it didn't matter. Kenny did not want to talk. He wasn't sure he wanted to fight either, not with his cold. He opened his mouth to let out a huge roar but sneezed instead. He could feel his face turning red.

The guard didn't move as Kenny stepped closer. The sword in the guard's hand held steady in front of him. He stood as if he was a skilled and experienced soldier. Kenny drew near to the man, ready to fight. It would be an easy battle.

He came in close to the soldier's face. It was time to scare the soldier and teach him a lesson for getting in Kenny's way.

He was about to attack when he noticed something. The guard's eyes were closed.

Kenny leaned in close and listened. He could hear snoring. The guard was sleepwalking!

"Hark! Who goes there?" The guard yelled out again, causing Kenny to jump a little.

The snore grew louder.

Kenny was mad. All of this to find the guy was sound asleep! He wanted to let out a roar and attack the man, but to do this would wake the man from his sleep. He couldn't do that. That would be rude.

He took a step to the side and tried to squeeze around the guard. Kenny was big, and the corridor wasn't huge. It was a tight squeeze, but he could make it. When he was nearly past the guard, the man started to stumble around, and Kenny had to jump and dance to avoid hitting the man and waking him. He could feel another kitten sneeze coming on and just barely managed to get past the man and around the corner before an adorable little sneeze came out again.

He shook his head and carried on. It was time to get the key and get out before someone awake heard him sneeze.

1. Liam and Harry

Liam ran for his life. If he couldn't keep ahead of the footsteps behind him, he wasn't sure he would live to see tomorrow. Harry was mad. Really mad.

Liam continued to run. Not only was Harry mad, but he was also fast. There wasn't a kid at school who could outrun him once he was at full speed. He could move! Harry's weakness, however, was his start. Harry would always start out slow. He would take a few steps and then begin to gain speed. Each step would carry him faster and faster. Once he was at full speed, there was no way to stop him.

The only hope anyone had was to change direction. Each time someone turned, Harry would have to take the time to pick up speed again.

Liam heard the pound of Harry's feet close behind him and turned sharply to his left down a side street. He heard Harry fly past him. The big guy had narrowly missed his target. It would take Harry a moment to bring himself to a stop and then figure out where Liam had gone. Then Harry would need some time to pick up speed again.

Liam wasn't far from home. He had run all the way from school, and he was exhausted. He never got used to these daily chases. If he could only make it home, he would be safe. Harry seemed to have a great deal of trouble figuring out which house was Liam's. They lived right next door to each other, but Harry wasn't the brightest guy in the world. Once Liam was out of sight, Harry struggled to remember where Liam lived. He had to get home.

Liam pushed his legs a little harder. He thought he could make it when he heard Harry's footsteps approach again from behind. He must have managed to turn around quickly and start running after Liam again.

Liam turned sharply down a side path. He couldn't remember where this path went but assumed it would come out somewhere, and he'd be able to find his way home from there.

As he ran down the path, something odd happened. He felt a strong pull. He wasn't sure what it was, but it made him feel as though he needed to go somewhere. He pushed the thought out of his mind. Now wasn't the time. He had more important things to worry about.

Harry came upon the path Liam had turned down, but he didn't quite make the turn. Liam heard him slam into the fence which lined the side of the path. Liam smiled to himself, but he knew he would pay for that one. He was sure of it.

The path continued past the two houses and opened up to a little park. It was a nice park. The grass was well cared for. There were swings, a slide and some climbing equipment. It was also safe for children to play here in the sense that a fence surrounded the entire park. The only way in or out was the path he had just come through. This was not good for Liam.

Liam came to a stop and scanned the outer rim of the park again just to make sure. There was no way out. The wooden fence around the outside was tall. Liam might be able to climb it, but it would slow him down enough that Harry would be able to catch him.

Liam heard the footsteps behind him come to a stop. He turned around, and Harry stood in the entrance, blocking the only way in or out of the park. He walked up close enough for Liam to smell him. Harry normally smelled of onions or garlic. Today was garlic.

Harry stared at him for a moment. Liam had always been one of Harry's favorite targets.

He stepped close and stood only a step or two away. He was about four inches taller than Liam and roughly forty pounds heavier. After that run, he didn't even seem to be breathing heavy. This kid was a tank!

He bared his teeth and spoke up, "Hello, Ed."

The first few months after Liam had met Harry, he had thought Harry was somehow trying to make fun of him by calling him "Ed." Liam didn't know what was funny about the name "Ed," but assumed Harry meant it to be mean. In time, however, Liam came to believe Harry honestly thought Liam's name was "Ed." No amount of evidence seemed to convince Harry it could be anything else. From the first day they'd met, six years ago, when Liam had moved into his house and bumped into his next-door neighbor Harry, he had consistently called Liam, "Ed."

"Hello, Harry. Nice day for a run."

Harry growled. He looked at Liam as though he needed a moment to figure out how best to torture him.

Liam started to feel the same pull he had felt earlier. This time it felt like his whole body was being sucked somewhere. He put out a foot in the direction of the pull to steady himself and focused back on Harry. Whatever it was, he had more important things to deal with at the moment.

Liam had tried to stand up to Harry many times over the years. He had tried to fight back, but Harry was too strong. He had tried to outrun him, but Harry was too fast. Sometimes he found he could talk his way out of the situation. That was his plan this time. He had prepared something new for today.

Liam had learned the key to talking his way out of an encounter with Harry was to confuse him. If Harry could make sense of everything, he would get bored and turn back to his favorite activity: torturing Liam. If Liam could confuse him just a little bit, he might be able to get away.

"Did you hear about Liam?" Liam asked. There were few things Harry liked more than picking on other kids, but one of them was gossip.

Harry's face lit up with excitement. He grabbed Liam by the shoulders and pulled him in close. Their noses almost touched as he yelled, "Tell me, Ed!"

The best way to confuse Harry was to talk about someone Harry didn't think existed. The perfect person to talk about, then, was Liam. Harry didn't appear to know a Liam, only an "Ed."

"Liam broke his leg."

Harry looked upset. Liam suspected it wasn't out of concern for this "Liam," but because Harry hadn't been involved.

"How did he break his leg?"

"He fell up his basement stairs at home."

Liam gave Harry a moment or two for him to absorb this answer. He could see confusion in Harry's eyes as he tried to make sense of it all. This was good.

"He fell… up… the stairs?"

"Yah! Of course, not just one flight. That would be silly. He fell up from the basement, rolled all the way into the kitchen, down the hallway and up to the second floor. The poor guy looks terrible.

He's covered in bruises. The doctors think he won't walk again for thousands of minutes."

Liam had prepared all this a few days before. He hoped it would confuse Harry long enough to give him a chance to get away.

Harry looked upset again. His face dropped, and he looked down at the ground. Liam was pretty sure he saw a tear form in one of Harry's eyes. He didn't know what to do.

"Uh, Harry?"

"Yah, Ed?"

"You okay?"

"Well, I'm just kinda sad, you know? I had planned to meet up with Liam later on today. I was going to maybe beat him up or something."

Liam was now confused. "You were going to do what?"

"Yah, I had him in my schedule." He pulled out a little book and showed Liam his weekly planner. He noticed "Ed" was written on each page. Sure enough, later that day, Harry had the name "Leeum" written in for the evening with the words, "beet upp" scribbled underneath.

Liam started to suspect things were about to turn out poorly for him. It was easier to talk about someone Harry didn't seem to know. Who was this other Liam?

He had forgotten all about the pull when it ramped up again. Liam thought he could feel himself slide a little bit on the ground. This was getting weird.

Harry growled again, and it brought Liam's thoughts back to the danger he faced. Harry's jaw tightened, and he looked at Liam like he was mad. "Ed! You tell Liam I want to meet him right here at lunchtime today. I don't care if he has a broken leg. He will meet me here or else!"

Things were starting to turn out poorly. Harry didn't take kindly to people who didn't do what he told them. Liam didn't know if there even was another Liam. He certainly couldn't bring him here.

Even if he could find another Liam willing to come, that other Liam probably didn't have a broken leg, and then the real Liam would have to explain that one. On top of this, Harry wanted this "Liam" kid here at lunchtime. It was already about four in the afternoon. There was no way Liam could survive this one.

Liam looked down to see his feet start to slide. The invisible force was dragging him toward the side of the park! He tried to plant his feet firmly on the ground and leaned off to the side away from the pull.

Harry didn't seem to notice anything out of the ordinary at first. He continued, "If you don't get him here in time, Ed, I'll fight you instead. Uh, Ed, what are you doing?"

Liam looked down. He was at a perfect forty-five-degree angle. He knew enough about gravity to know that he should fall right about now. Whatever was pulling him was strong.

Harry looked worried. He walked around beside Liam and stared at him on an angle. Harry was not good at things like angles or gravity or intelligent thought, but he knew enough to see that something wasn't quite right.

Liam reached down and grabbed hold of a clump of grass on the ground to try to keep himself in place. The pull grew stronger. He started to slip, and Harry laughed as he watched Liam dragged by some unseen force over the grass of the park and toward one of the fences.

Liam hit the fence and came to a stop. The force which had taken hold of him couldn't seem to pull him through the fence. Liam was happy about that.

"Harry, something weird is happening. Go get help!"

Harry looked at Liam for a moment before shaking his head. "No, Ed. I think this is for the best."

"What? What are you talking about? What's for the best? I've been pulled into a fence by an invisible force!"

"Whatever is holding you there is going to help me." Harry smiled and charged at Liam.

Liam yelled. This was going to hurt! Harry ran as fast as he could toward him. He quickly closed the gap between them. Liam couldn't budge from his position.

Just as Harry was about to hit him, Liam felt the pull grow stronger, and he slid up the fence and over the top. He heard the crash where Harry had hit the boards, but he had more important things on his mind. He hit the ground and slid through someone's backyard. He then slid between two houses and out toward the street. Once out front, the force pulling his body turned him, and he slid down the sidewalk. He could see he wasn't far from home.

He rounded a corner and saw his house up ahead. Some of his neighbors were outside. He hollered for help, but most just took pictures with their phones and yelled that this was the coolest thing they had ever seen.

He slid across the front lawn of his house and up the front steps. He slammed against the front door. Whatever pulled him wanted him in the house. He reached for the handle and slowly turned it. The door flew open, and he tumbled in. The force pulled him down the hallway and into the kitchen.

His parents were both in the kitchen as usual, hard at work baking. Today Liam smelled chocolate chip cookies. There were what looked like fifty dozen cookies all piled up on the counter.

Liam grabbed the counter and held on for dear life. He looked over to see his parents staring at him with a look of curiosity on their faces. He realized this must have been quite the sight. He held onto the counter with both hands, his body and legs extended straight out about three feet above the floor.

His dad spoke up first, "Hmm… that's unusual. You don't normally suspend yourself above the floor like that, Liam, do you?"

"No, Dad, this is new for me," Liam replied.

"How was school, dear?" Liam's mom asked.

Liam couldn't believe how relaxed they seemed about the whole, "Liam floating above the ground, held up by nothing but his two hands holding onto the counter" thing. He would have thought they would find this a little more unnerving.

"Help me! I'm being dragged somewhere by some unseen force!"

"That's nice, Liam. Glad school went well today," his mom responded before both parents turned back to the cookies. Liam lost his grip on the counter and continued through the kitchen. On his way, he managed to grab a handful of cookies. He didn't know where he would end up but thought he would need to keep up his energy.

The pull dragged him up the stairs and around the corner. He slid down the hallway and grabbed the doorframe of his bedroom. He held on for a moment and peered inside the room. He was instantly hit by the smell of dirty clothes and poor ventilation. The room looked like someone had gone through everything he owned, dumped out his drawers and tossed everything around. He was comforted to know at least his room was the same as always.

He lost his grip and slid farther down the hallway toward the bathroom. The door was open, and he could see the toilet straight ahead. As he was dragged closer, he looked in horror as the toilet seat slowly raised. Somehow, he knew this pull was dragging him toward the toilet. He cried out in fear. He didn't know what was going on, but he knew he did not want to be flushed. He wondered if he could even fit down the toilet drain. He suddenly had an image flash in his mind of a plumber explaining to his parents that there was a thirteen-year-old boy clogging their toilet drain.

As he entered the bathroom, he grabbed for the doorframe. The whole room turned into a windstorm, and he could see that inside the toilet was a swirl of colors. Liam began to scream for help. He hoped someone could hear him above the wind.

The wind grabbed his feet. It pulled one foot into the toilet. Liam imagined his obituary: "Liam, died thirteen years old, sucked into a toilet. Death by flushing. A fitting end for such a young life."

By this time, both feet were well into the toilet. He called again for help, but no one seemed to hear. His fingers held on as long as they could, but his grip began to weaken. With one last yell, Liam went in. His whole body disappeared down the drain. He had been flushed.

2. Ezra

Liam held his breath... not just because of the water in the toilet, but because of how gross the thought was of having his mouth open while being sucked down a toilet. Oddly enough, the thought that went through his mind was, "Why do I have to die this way?" There was a sense of injustice to the whole thing. Liam felt no one should ever have to go this way.

Everything went dark for a moment, and he could feel only the rush of movement—a movement one would not expect to feel while using the toilet. The world was cold, and he felt confused. Liam realized not only was he not breathing, but he could not sense any of his limbs. He began to feel a new level of panic.

Light exploded all around him, and solid ground quickly came up to meet him. He wondered what he could do to make the crash into the ground hurt less. He continued to wonder this as his body crashed into the ground. It hurt a lot. He tumbled across the

11

hard-packed dirt, each twist and turn adding to his pain. He came to a full stop, closed his eyes and laid there for a moment.

He wiggled his toes, then his fingers, content that they were still there and still worked. He wrinkled his nose. The smell was horrible, but not unexpected considering he had just been flushed down a toilet.

He decided to risk it. He would open his eyes to see where he was. There was no doubt about it, he would be in the sewer and have to live out the rest of his years with four goldfish and three sets of his dad's keys, all of which he knew were down here somewhere. He hoped his parents would figure out where he was and start to flush edible snacks down the toilet for him.

He cracked open both eyes and stared up at the blue sky. A few clouds slowly floated by. He could feel a gentle, warm breeze on his skin. It appeared peaceful. A bird flew overhead, some kind of eagle or other majestic bird. It circled a couple of times, appeared to take aim and dropped a little present for Liam.

Liam rolled out of the way just in time to protect his head from the splat. He looked around and saw the source of the stink he had smelled. He had landed in the middle of a dirt road, in the middle of a town. He looked around to see horse-drawn carriages as they moved back and forth. The source of the smell was droppings left by the horses.

"Where am I?" Liam asked to no one in particular as he got to his feet. "And what is this place?"

He turned to head over toward a group of men and women who stood off to the side of the road. He hoped to find some answers. As he walked, something crashed into him, and the world went sideways. Liam rolled head over heels about six times before he came to a stop in a tangled mess with another young man.

"Hi, I'm Ezra!" His new "friend" seemed happy to chat as they both lay on the ground. "If you don't want to be associated with

12

me, we'd better untangle ourselves, and you'd better stand far apart from me!"

"What? Associated with you? What are you talking about?" Liam stuttered.

"HALT!" Everyone in the street, including the horses, instantly came to a stop and no one made a single noise. Liam looked and saw a group of guards dressed in dirty, ugly armor. They drew their swords as they moved toward Liam and Ezra from down the street. "There's his accomplice. Arrest them both!"

"Too late! I guess they are now associating you with me. If you want to live, you'd better run." Ezra jumped up, pulled Liam to his feet and started to run into an alley.

Liam stopped and tried to think through his situation for a moment. He wasn't too keen on following this 'Ezra' down a dark alley, but those guards didn't look like they cared whether or not Liam was a part of whatever Ezra had been up to. Add to that the fact that Liam really didn't know what was going on and that he was pretty sure those guards were not people he wanted to meet, he felt he had no choice but to follow.

Liam bolted down the alleyway behind Ezra.

The alley led between a series of buildings, some of which were houses, others appeared to be stores. He ran down the alley, careful of his step. He didn't want to land in one of the puddles on the ground as he wasn't sure it was water they held. He jumped over each of these, dodged an elderly lady and skirted around the occasional rabid-looking dog or feral cat.

"Ezra! Wait! Why are they chasing you?" Liam called out.

Ezra came to a stop, and Liam slammed into him. His new friend turned around and looked Liam in the eye. "You should stop for a moment and think that question through. I think you want to ask, 'Why are they chasing us?'." With that, he turned and bolted around a corner into a busy street.

Liam ran after him. "Okay, why are they chasing us?"

Ezra hollered back, "Good job! Now you're understanding the situation! They are chasing us because they want to catch us. I don't think they would be able to catch us if they didn't chase us. I think that should be pretty obvious." He then swerved across the street and turned down another alley.

Liam turned the corner to follow Ezra and came to a dead end. Ezra was nowhere in sight. He looked around for a way out. He started to think he'd never see this Ezra again when two hands popped out from behind a pile of broken boards and pulled him through.

"Follow me!" whispered Ezra as he began crawling beneath what appeared to be a series of houses. "Keep your voice down, or the people who live in these houses will report us."

Liam crawled. He occasionally glanced up through the rather large cracks between the floorboards. In one house, he witnessed a lady juggle three mangy cats. Two of the cats purred while the third cleaned itself. In another, a gentleman knit a sweater for what appeared to be a rather large horse. In a third, two children sat on the floor. They argued over whether or not carrots felt pain.

As he crawled and looked through the cracks, Liam missed the fact that Ezra had stopped crawling and had come to a halt. He ran headfirst into Ezra's butt. "Hey, watch it!" Ezra whispered. He dropped down onto his belly and slithered out from under the building and stopped alongside a watering trough for horses.

Liam followed close behind and took in where they were. They looked out over a large marketplace. There were hundreds of booths spread out over just about every square inch of the place. There were even booths stacked on top of one another. For the two-level booths, buyers stood below the seller and threw money up as items such as cloth, vegetables, toys and more were dropped down to the buyers. There were also street performers such as jugglers and fire-breathers, puppet masters and acrobats.

Liam was filled with such awe at what he saw. He had never witnessed anything quite like this. It took a chicken trying to swallow his nose to pull him back.

"Wha??? Ezra, there's a chicken trying to eat my nose." He pulled at it for a moment before saying, "He won't let go."

Ezra calmly looked over at Liam as if this happened all the time.

"Jep!" Ezra said to the chicken. "We've talked about this. You cannot eat people's noses while they are attached to their face."

Jep looked a little embarrassed, but still did not release the firm hold his beak had on Liam's nose. He squawked a reply to Ezra while he continued to clamp down.

Liam had never seen a chicken look embarrassed before. He had also never seen a chicken bite someone's nose, let alone get nearly the entire nose between its beak. As uncomfortable as Liam was, he was somewhat impressed.

"Let him go, Jep!" Ezra sounded like he meant business and the chicken tried to release but seemed to have some trouble detaching.

After a couple failed attempts to release his bite, Liam noticed the chicken was acting funny. It started to make a few odd noises. At first, he didn't know what was happening, but then he figured it out.

"The chicken's about to puke!" Liam hissed! "Get him off me now!"

Ezra didn't seem to pick up on the urgency of the situation. Although it had never occurred to him to worry about such a thing, Liam was sure he did not want to experience a chicken barf up his nose. Ezra slowly started into action. He reached for Jep to try to get him off Liam before it was too late.

"Hurry before I..." Liam wasn't sure what he would do, but he needed this chicken off his nose immediately!

Ezra, unfortunately, seemed quite curious about what Liam might do. "You know, I'm willing to hurry, but you need to finish that sentence! Leaving a sentence half-finished is like…" Liam waited and then got the picture.

"Hurry before I get chicken puke up my nose!"

"Ahh, that makes sense. Why didn't you just say that?" Ezra reached over and detached the gagging chicken from Liam's face.

Liam looked down at the chicken. He was about the size of a normal rooster. "Why was he doing that?" Liam was sure the chicken smiled at him.

"Why was he doing that?" Ezra asked. "Wouldn't you start to gag if you had someone's nose in your mouth?"

"No, I mean why did he bite my nose?"

"No time for that now. We have to move." Ezra appeared ready to take charge. "It seems to me that if we can make it across the market without being spotted by one of the guards, we should be okay. I think if we charge right through the market screaming as loud as we can that everyone should look the other way, we'll get through without being seen."

Liam wasn't one to criticize a plan right away. He always liked to encourage other people and build them up for their ideas. He liked to emphasize the strengths of a suggestion and downplay the weaknesses. But this time there didn't seem to be any way to be gentle.

"That plan stinks, Ezra."

Ezra looked over at Liam with a look of confusion on his face. "You see some flaws in my plan?"

Liam decided to take another approach. "What if we kind of hide our faces and try to sneak across the market quietly. Maybe we will go unnoticed."

"What's your name?" Ezra asked.

"Liam."

"Okay, Liam. Think this through. If we try to act like we don't want to be seen, don't you think we're just going to draw attention to ourselves? YOUR plan stinks! I think someone who just recently couldn't pull a chicken from his nose shouldn't be so critical of another person's plans. When we stand up and scream, "Look the other way," everyone is going to look the other way! It's the perfect plan. Don't you know anything about people?"

With that, Ezra stood up in the market and screamed, "Don't look at me! Look the other way!"

To Liam's amazement, everyone looked away. Some even covered their eyes. There were even guards in the middle of the marketplace, and they put their hands over their eyes or held shields up so they couldn't see.

Liam watched Ezra run. He screamed his way right through the market and into a doorway on the other side. These people were nuts! Wherever he was, it was an absolutely bizarre place. There was only one thing to do. Copy Ezra.

As Liam was about to stand up and scream for people to look the other way, Jep took advantage of the distraction and latched on again. There was no time to waste. The plan was in motion, and Liam refused to be stopped.

"Everyone look away, I have a chicken on my nose!" Everyone's faces went red in embarrassment and turned away. He screamed again, "Look away, chicken-boy coming through!" As he ran, he could hear people saying, "Poor young man. How will he survive with a chicken on his nose?"

Liam zigzagged through the non-lookers and found his way to the same door Ezra had charged through. By this time his nose hurt a lot, but he decided to wait until he saw Ezra again to get his help in dealing with the nose-biter.

As he closed the door behind him, he could hear the crowds get back to buying and selling as though nothing at all out of the ordinary had happened. He looked around and took in the sights and sounds and smells of this new place.

The room was dark and small. The entire house (aside from a bathroom) seemed to be in this one room. There were two bunk beds built into the one wall to his right, one a total disaster as if it had just been used and another neat and tidy. Next to the bunks on the back wall was what appeared to be a small kitchen area with a stove that could clearly heat the place as well as cook food. Up against the left wall was a small table with three chairs set next to it.

In one of the chairs sat Ezra; in another sat a most disagreeable-looking creature. She had curly, matted hair which stuck out in every direction. Liam couldn't see her eyes through the thick mess of tangled eyebrows. The hands were more claw than anything with sharp nails and hooked fingers. As the creature sized up Liam, it began to let out a terrifying cackle.

Liam stood there with the chicken still attached to his very sore nose. He was pretty sure Ezra had just led him to his death.

3. Soup Lady

The creature at the table lunged at Liam and pinned him up against the wall. From the light that came through the closed shutters over the windows, Liam could see it wasn't a creature. It was an elderly woman with a huge amount of dark hair. At least Liam thought she was elderly. It was hard to see her face through all the hair.

She leaned in close and whispered something in Jep's ear, and the chicken released its hold again. It flapped over to her shoulder.

The woman stared up at Liam as if she was sizing him up. She was a rather short lady wearing what appeared to be about six different layers of clothing. Her face was quite round and had an angry look to it. Her skin was covered in bumps and warts and the occasional hairy mole. The color of her teeth alternated green and yellow from one to the next. What stood out the most, however, were her eyebrows. Liam suspected she had more hair matted together in those eyebrows than he had on his entire head. There was so much hair in those brows, he could not, in fact, actually see her eyes through them.

"I think you're right, Ezra. He's a traveler."

"Yep, he sure is, Masha."

"Good… good." Masha released her hold on Liam and started to walk away with Jep on her shoulder. As she walked, she continued to whisper, "good… good…" under her breath. She had a voice like a growl, and it only added to the scary vibe she was giving off.

"What does it mean that I am a traveler? And why is that good?" Liam was quite nervous about being there in that house but didn't want to take his chances with the guards. He wasn't sure where he would be safest.

"Be quiet!!" The woman screamed and ran at Liam, pinning him to the wall again. "If you don't stop all your yabbering, I'm going to get Jep to bite your nose again!"

Liam looked at Jep sitting on her shoulder and realized he was ready to go at any moment.

"Okay, I'm good. I'm a traveler," Liam said. He was used to dealing with Harry and talking his way out of dangerous situations. He could roll with this one. Everything was so strange here. He couldn't help but think that just a few minutes ago, he was standing face to face with Harry in the park. Now he was trying to figure out how to deal with guards chasing him through some strange medieval town, a nose-biting chicken and a short, hairy and quite fearsome woman pinning him against the wall.

"That's right… good… good…" Masha released him and started to walk away again.

Liam sat down at the table next to Ezra. He sized up his new friend. He was a little shorter than Liam—probably a year or so younger. He had dark brown skin, tight curly dark brown hair and a look in his eye that suggested to Liam a thirst for adventure.

"So, Ezra," Liam whispered so as not to bring down the wrath of the hairy woman again. "I don't know what's going on. I don't even know how I got here." He stopped for a moment and took a deep breath. "I don't even know where 'here' is."

Ezra leaned over and put his hand on Liam's arm. "It's okay. I'll explain everything. You're not the first person to come and visit us in our world. I'll bring you up to speed. We get travelers like you all the time. But first, let's have some soup."

Liam looked up just in time to see two rather large eyebrows descend on his position. A bowl of soup plopped down before him and one before Ezra. The soup looked disgusting. In fact, it looked like Liam would not be able to stomach it and he wondered if he could dispose of it without Eyebrows knowing.

The woman looked angrily at Liam and hollered, "I'm Masha! I live here! I make soup! Good soup! You will eat it now!"

With that, something happened. It took Liam a few moments to wrap his mind around what was going on. He didn't think it was possible, but this Masha somehow managed to smoothly grab hold of both Liam and Ezra's tongues with her fingers and yank their heads down to their bowls. She held them in place and yelled, "You will eat soup now!"

Liam wondered how she managed to get her hand into his mouth and grip his tongue without any trouble at all. He struggled and tried to pull away, but her grip was like iron. He thought a tongue was wet and slippery so he should just be able to pull it out, but he was locked down in the bowl of soup.

He tried to look over at Ezra and found a certain satisfaction as he saw Ezra struggle as well. However, he noticed that Ezra didn't seem upset at having his face held down in his soup by Masha. He struggled to eat but seemed fine with the whole arrangement. There was no panic in his eyes; this was simply normal for him. Liam

21

realized the only way out was to have the bowl empty of soup. He began to eat, as best he could with his tongue gripped firmly by an elderly lady's fingers.

When he had finished the soup, or at least as much as he could with his face held in his bowl, Masha let go, scooped up the bowls and stormed away. She seemed happy in her anger or perhaps satisfied her soup was gobbled up with such effort.

Liam's face was absolutely covered in soup. He looked around. There was nothing within reach he could use to clean up, so he wiped his face with his sleeve.

Ezra, on the other hand, reached down, grabbed Jep with his hands and, to Jep's dismay, used the chicken as a towel to wipe his face. He set Jep down and watched as the chicken scurried away looking very unhappy.

Liam looked at Ezra and waited for an explanation about the soup experience. Ezra, however, simply leaned back in his chair and gave no indication this was anything out of the ordinary. He decided it was best to ignore the experience and move on to where he was and what was going on.

"Ezra, where am I and how can I get back home?"

"Well, that's a long story. I suggest we move over by the fireplace while we chat."

Liam looked at the fireplace. In this tiny, one-room house, it was right next to him. He realized he couldn't move any closer to the fireplace without actually moving into it. Ezra simply turned in his chair a bit, seemed satisfied that they were close to the fireplace and began his tale.

"Every now and then a traveler shows up around the city. This has been going on for years. They arrive and are confused about where they are. They never seem to know how they got here or why they are here. Each traveler is here for a time and has a quest they must fulfill before they are able to return to wherever they came from."

"So, what's my quest?" Liam thought if he could get this figured out and taken care of quickly, he might make it back in time for supper tonight.

"I have no idea! How am I supposed to know? Maybe it's to defeat a dragon; maybe you need to battle the evil Chimpanzee army of Rice Pudding Lake; maybe you need to climb a mountain and rescue a princess trapped at the top."

"Do you have a lot of princesses trapped on the top of mountains?" Liam wondered if Ezra was trying to trick him with this talk of Rice Pudding, Chimpanzee armies and the like.

"Of course we do! Just about every mountain has a princess on top, trapped in a cage or in ice or under a waterfall. It's the way mountains have always been!"

Liam was having a little trouble wrapping his mind around how strange this world was. How could having a princess trapped on top of a mountain be normal? For that matter, how could there be an army of chimpanzees? Everything here was strange to him, but maybe everything in his world would be strange to Ezra. He was beginning to realize his time in this world was not going to be easy.

"Okay, so how do we find out what my quest is?" Liam could feel frustration growing in him with Ezra and the whole situation. He also started to think this quest would take longer than he'd like.

"Usually the traveler just goes about his business and then the quest sort of presents itself. Sort of like how we met. You just ran into me."

"You ran into me!" Liam corrected.

"Details, details, just let me tell you about our world. You have entered the land called Snotworld. We are named this because of the great snot mines in the Booger Mountains not far from the capital city of Phlegm. The people of this land are called the Snots, although those of wealth and position are called Boogers, and the rest of us are called, Little Snots."

Liam stared in disbelief at Ezra for a moment. He then began to realize this was no less strange than anything else he'd experienced up until this point. He figured he should probably just listen for now.

Ezra continued, "So there is a country to the south of us who are our mortal enemies. They refuse to call this land Snotworld, but refer to this planet as "Hanky" and will often attack and seek to wipe out all the Little Snots. Back a few years ago, they made it through our defenses, and we had to flee into the Booger Mountains. There is a great keep there which we call the Clogged Sinuses, hidden behind a large waterfall we call, The Great Runny Nose."

"So, welcome to Snotworld!" Ezra wiped his nose with his hand and offered it to Liam.

Liam was so grossed out that he almost threw up his soup, but didn't want to be rude. He slowly took Ezra's now sticky hand and shook it.

Liam sat in silence for a moment or two. It all seemed strange to him. His head was spinning and every minute that passed made him miss home more. He had to start to make sense of some of this. "I just have one question. Why are all the princesses up on top of mountains?"

Ezra looked thoughtful for a moment. "You know, now that you mention it, that is kind of strange. I mean, where would they get new dresses to wear each day? No princess is going to wear the same outfit two days in a row."

"Really, Ezra? Really? That's the only thing that seems strange about each mountain having a captive princess on top of it?"

Ezra stared back at Liam for a moment as though he found it difficult to understand Liam's question. After a moment he simply continued. "So, Snotworld is normally ruled by a king. This king is chosen by a magical box in the castle. After a king dies, they use the special key and open the box. In the box, each time a new king is needed, a note appears with the new king's name and that person rules till they die."

"Normally? You mean that's not the case right now?" Liam asked.

"Normally that's the case, but right now they seem to have misplaced the key for the box. The king died last year, and no one knows how to open the box without the key. So Smeetho, that was the royal advisor, stepped up and named himself Regent until the key is found and the new king is named. The king rules in the castle in the center of this city and the city's name is, Kings-Home."

"Kings-Home? That's not overly creative." Liam didn't want to be difficult, but this was a lot to take in, and he was feeling very irritable.

"What do you mean?" Ezra asked.

"Kings-Home! Home of the King! Don't you think you could have come up with a more creative name for the city?" The frustration with everything that had happened today from his run-ins with Harry to being sucked down a toilet into another world to everything here in Snotworld had brought Liam to a point where politeness was no longer important to him.

"I don't follow you," Ezra replied.

"AAAAAAHHHHH!!! Kings-Home? Home of the King? This is the King's Home?"

"Ohh… when you put it that way it makes perfect sense, doesn't it Masha?" Ezra looked over at Masha with a look that seemed to say, 'Just go with it… this traveler may not be all here.'

In response, Masha screamed something unintelligible at Liam and brandished the soup ladle at him in a threatening manner.

Liam decided to drop it. He knew he was in a world where many ways of doing things and ways of thinking were completely different than his world. He would just have to learn to roll with it.

Just then the door burst open. An old man leapt into the room and screamed, "Where's my soup???"

4. Jrasta

The man who stood in the doorway was average height but very thin. He was breathing heavy, hunched over a little bit and had about a week's worth of beard growth. His hair was part black, part white and hung just below his shoulders. The hair looked like it hadn't been washed. Perhaps not ever.

His clothes were dirty and had many rips and patches. Some of his patches even had rips in them. His shoes, however, were very odd. They looked brand new and shiny black as though he shined them every single day. This in and of itself was odd compared with the rest of the outfit, but what made it really strange were the toes. All ten toes were sticking out holes in the front of the shoes. It was like a pair of fingerless gloves, but for feet. As he spoke, his toes wiggled, and Liam found it quite distracting.

"WHERE'S MY SOUP?!?!" the toe wiggler screamed again.

Liam didn't think Masha could move quite so fast. She crossed the room, elbowed Liam in the side of the head on her way, grabbed the man's tongue in her left hand and dragged him back to the table where there was a bowl of soup already set out for him. On the way back to the table, she managed to elbow Liam in the side of the head again. Liam couldn't help but notice Masha had gone out of her way each time to elbow him.

Masha grabbed Liam with her free hand and tossed him out of his chair, seating the man in Liam's now vacant seat. He wanted to ask why she didn't use the empty third chair but feared to get involved.

Liam watched in horror as the man ate the soup with his tongue held firmly in the bowl by Masha. It appeared to be just as horrible to watch as it was to experience, but just like Ezra, the man did not seem to be surprised in the least at the whole "grab the tongue, eat the soup" thing.

Liam made his way over to the empty chair and sat down. He tried to be quiet and stay out of the way for a moment. This was all a lot to take in.

After a messy meal, Masha let go of the man's tongue, and he stood up. He grabbed a clump of her hair and wiped his face clean. Masha smiled in approval.

After he finished his quick cleanup, he turned his attention to Liam.

"And who do we have here?" grumbled the old man.

"I'm Liam. I'm a traveler, I guess. I'm from Earth."

"You come from the earth? Like a worm?"

"No, I mean the planet is called…"

"Quiet, Worm-Boy! It's time for me to speak and you to listen. My name is Jrasta! It is an absolute pleasure to meet you and an even greater pleasure for you to meet me! Let me tell you about our world. This planet is called Snotworld, and each of us are the Little Snots. I am a particularly important Snot, so sometimes they even call me a Booger. Our planet is named Snotworld because of the…"

"Yah, yah, yah, we covered that," Ezra piped up. "I told him all about the world and how he has to find his quest and so on."

"All about it? There's nothing left to tell?" The man looked quite disappointed as if Ezra had stolen something very precious from him. Liam thought this was odd but was beginning to think all things here were odd.

"Well, that's no fun!" The man walked over to the chair Liam was sitting in, rolled Liam out of it onto the floor and sat down. Jrasta stuck out his bottom lip and began to pout.

Liam wasn't sure how to respond but thought he would try to be polite. "It's nice to meet you, Draw-sta."

The man looked at him with his bottom lip still stuck out. "It's pronounced 'Jra-sta.' 'Jra' like the first part of giraffe. Jrasta."

Liam felt a little comfort in that. This was a strange world, but at least they had giraffes here. He wasn't sure why that made him feel better, but it was nice to know they had something here he was familiar with. It made him feel a little less homesick. He had never actually seen a giraffe up close, though. "Do you have giraffes around here?"

Masha hollered out, "Of course we do, Worm-Boy! Here, have one!"

With that, she threw something small, hard and round at him. It hit him in the chest and knocked the wind out of him. When he looked down at the floor to see what she had thrown, he saw what looked like an apple. He picked it up and took a bite. It was an apple.

"You call this a giraffe?"

Ezra piped up, "Of course! What do you call it in your world, worm food?" Everyone laughed at Liam for that one. Ezra then turned to Masha, "You're not going to leave him in those clothes, are you, Masha? He looks like a ragamuffin. Don't you have something

29

appropriate he can wear?" Ezra looked disdainfully at Liam and his outfit.

"I have some of DOHNK's clothes. You man enough to wear a dress, boy?" Masha eyed Liam with something close to disdain.

"I'm not wearing a dress," Liam declared. It was time to put his foot down, and this was his moment to take a stand. He wasn't sure what was wrong with his clothes, but they were a very different style than what Ezra was wearing.

"Well, I have boy clothes as well, but it's a pity to waste them on you." Masha trudged off toward a small cupboard at the head of her bed. She opened the latch, climbed headfirst into the cupboard and disappeared. A few moments later, a mange of curly hair appeared, and Masha came out with a set of really old, stinky clothes for Liam.

"Put them on, Worm-Boy!" Masha screamed. She grabbed a curtain from the wall and pulled it out, forming a small area just big enough for someone to change privately. Liam stepped inside and changed into the clothes. They appeared to fit perfectly, although they looked older than Jrasta.

He pulled back the curtain and stepped out in his new outfit. He looked up just in time to see Masha lunge for him. Before he could stop her, she grabbed his old clothes and threw them into the stove.

"What are you doing?" Liam hollered.

"I'm burning your clothes!" Masha hollered back. She turned to Jrasta, "I think this worm-boy has poor eyesight. Go easy on him." She grabbed a candle off a shelf and lit a sleeve from Liam's shirt. His clothes caught fire immediately, and within seconds there was nothing left.

"My eyes are fine!" Liam countered, but no one listened.

Liam slumped against a wall and looked around the small room. He was mad, upset and very confused. He wanted to scream and cry and laugh all at the same time. He thought doing that might cause him to fit in a little better with this crowd. Suddenly the nose eating chicken seemed the most normal one around. He decided he'd better start to try to make sense of the situation.

"Ezra, why were the guards chasing you?"

"Hmm… that's a good question. I don't know."

"How can you not know why they were chasing you? Did you break the law?"

"Yes, of course I did." Ezra looked at Liam like he was out of his mind.

"Well then, wouldn't that be the reason they are chasing you?" Liam wondered if he was in for another really stupid conversation.

"Yes, I would think that would make sense."

"So, what did you do?"

Ezra looked at Liam with complete sincerity and said, "I have no idea."

Liam closed his eyes and shook his head. He looked at Ezra and tried to get some more information. "So you did break the law, but you don't know why they were chasing you? You know they are chasing you because you broke the law, but YOU DON'T KNOW WHY THEY ARE CHASING YOU?!" Liam was beyond frustration. He just decided that there must be some reason behind all this nonsense.

"Let me spell it out for you clearly," Ezra responded.

Liam leaned in close to hear the first clear answer he thought Ezra may have ever given.

"I… don't… know…"

Liam wasn't surprised. "Really? That's it? You just don't know? You don't know what?"

"I don't know. I know that they are chasing me because I broke the law. I know that's why they chase me each time they chase me. I just don't know why they are chasing me this time. Was it because I stole some food, broke into the blacksmith's stable, set fire to the candy store? Was it because I painted the jail a nice shade of blue in the middle of the night last Tuesday? Was it because this morning I released thirty-four piglets into the guardhouse over on Butcher's Row? Oh, wait, that was probably it. Come to think of it, they actually said to me, 'We'll catch you and throw you in jail for this.' Yep, that's probably it."

Liam buried his face in his hands. The frustration of all of this was building. Add to the fact that he couldn't get out of this world until this "quest" or whatever was completed and he just wanted to scream.

He took a couple deep breaths and started to think matters through. He could flip out, scream and yell and tell them their whole world was too snotty for his taste. He could try to find someone else who might be a little easier to talk to. He could simply just give in and enter into their little insane world and live out his days here. Or, he could figure out the quest, complete it and go home. That seemed like the best option.

Turning to Ezra, he said, "Ezra, I need to figure out what my quest is. I'm wondering if I won't be able to figure it out while I'm sitting here. Can you take me somewhere where I might be able to find out what I'm supposed to do? I want to get back home as soon as possible."

While Liam spoke, a very mischievous looking smile broke out on Ezra's face. "Now you're talkin'! The first thing we need to do is get back out on the streets where the guards can catch us. It's too boring in here, and we're not going to find our quest unless we're on the move." With that, Ezra stood up, grabbed Liam by the shoulders, swung open the door and pushed him out.

Liam landed on his hands and knees in mud—at least he hoped it was mud—but that wasn't the worst part. The worst part was that a matter of inches from Liam's nose was a pair of armored boots. He feared they belonged to a soldier. In seconds he was on his feet, held firmly by two guards, while the third clapped him in irons.

A fourth guard, presumably the lead guard since he had the largest hat out of the four, looked on as the three secured Liam. "We've been searching the whole city for you, and then you simply throw yourself right at our feet! Now, where's your friend? The one who owns all those piglets?"

Before Liam could answer, a figure slammed into the guard. The guard tumbled to the ground. Ezra rolled to a stop beside the now very angry looking man. The look on Ezra's face showed that he was enjoying every part of this experience. The guard reached for Ezra as two more figures emerged from the door ready for battle. Jrasta, as old as he looked, moved so fast it was hard for Liam to take it all in. In moments two of the guards were on the ground, both disarmed. The second figure, Jep, attacked one of the guards on the ground, giving Ezra the help he needed with his much larger opponent.

Liam thought they might make it out of this situation when eight more guards rounded the corner and quickly put an end to the fight. In short order, all four were chained together in shackles, with Liam at the front, followed by Ezra, then Jrasta with Jep bringing up the tail.

The lead guard straightened up, brushed off his armor and commanded, "Search the house! See if they have any more accomplices!"

With that announcement, four guards began to make their way toward the shack but halted as Masha emerged.

"It's me in here! I'm the last one in this place." Masha stood there with a soup ladle in her hand. She looked surprisingly threatening standing before them in her apron.

"Hello, Masha. It's, uh, good to see you today. We're going to have to ask you to come with us." The lead guard seemed quite nervous of Masha.

"I'm not coming with you, Sergeant Dimwit," Masha declared in her angry voice. "I just made some soup, and I won't waste it. Which one of you wants to come in for soup?" With that offer, each soldier took a large step backward. Whether it was the taste of the soup or the tongue experience they feared, clearly Masha was well known by these men, and not one of them was willing to face her.

"It's, um, Sergeant Dimmock." The guard stood up straight and looked at Masha. She frowned back at him, and a look of fear passed over his face. "But Sergeant Dimwit is just fine. Thank you. But you'll still need to come with us."

Masha took a step forward and brandished her ladle.

Sergeant Dimmock took a step back, "Very well, then. If you won't come with us, we will be forced to move on."

Masha looked scornfully at the guard and slowly nodded her head. The guard nodded back and said, "Good day, Ma'am" before he turned to his prisoners and directed the guards to move.

Liam thought the day couldn't possibly get any worse. He had been sucked down a toilet, bit repeatedly by a chicken, force-fed soup, chased by guards, and now he had been arrested.

5. Arrested

The guards led the prisoners out of the market square and through the city. As they traveled, they passed a very nicely painted jail.

From behind Liam, Ezra piped up. "Wow! That's a mighty fine looking jail. I like the color. Kind of a nice sky blue, don't you think, Sarge? I wonder who painted that. Don't you wonder that, Sarge?"

"Silence, prisoner!" Sergeant Dimmock hollered back. "Someone painted it that color the other day, and when we catch him, he'll be sorry!"

They trudged on. A little farther down the street, Ezra poked Liam in the back and pointed to a burnt down building. Liam noticed there were children scattered throughout what was left of the building. They were licking the floors and walls. Ezra mumbled something under his breath about burning down the candy store and laughed to himself.

This was a very strange place. If he'd just met Ezra and Jrasta back in his world, he would have thought them simply to be odd, but the more he took in of this place it was clear the whole world was strange. Snotworld. With a name like that, what would one expect?

"Why am I being arrested?" Liam asked. He hoped to help the guard to see that he hadn't done anything wrong.

The Sergeant stopped and grabbed him by the collar. He yelled in his face, "You are not being arrested! You are already arrested. If we were currently arresting you, you could ask why you are being arrested because it would be happening at that moment, but you have already been arrested so the proper question to ask would be, 'Why have I been arrested?'"

Liam lifted his shackled hands up to his face and wiped a significant amount of guard spit from his cheeks and forehead. "Then why have I been arr…"

"Silence! No questions allowed! Certainly not from someone who has spit all over his face!" The guard pushed Liam forward, and the march continued.

Up ahead there was a rather large wooden gate with iron bands across it. The gate was set in a wall which encircled a large, stone building behind. Perhaps this was where the king lived, or the king would live when there was one.

Liam risked a glance back at Ezra. He had a big smile on his face and seemed to be absolutely thrilled with this whole experience. The boy clearly lived for adventure and didn't care what danger there may be. Liam thought he would be wise to find someone else to hang out with if he wanted to survive to the end of his quest.

As they approached the gate, the doors began to open. The guard paused briefly to explain to the soldiers at the door that he had four prisoners to present to the Regent and the procession moved on.

Inside the gate, there was a large courtyard. Off to the one side, there were squares marked out for sparring. There were a number of soldiers practicing sword fighting or hand to hand combat. Off to the other side was an archery range and a stable. Up ahead there were some smaller doors and gates leading into the main castle. It was through one of the smaller doors that the procession moved. As they entered, Liam looked around to see a dimly lit room with no features except a dark staircase. They moved toward the stairs and began to ascend. The stairs turned to the left as it led upwards. At the top there was a thin hallway with many doors; the one at the end was a rather large and fancy door.

The large door was extremely ornate in its design. It had carvings of fruits and vegetables, people in fancy dress, dragons and dog heads and animals Liam didn't recognize. In the center, there was a large iron door knocker. Sergeant Dimmock stepped up to the knocker, grabbed it with both hands and slammed it down once, creating a loud booming sound which echoed through the hall.

He howled out in agony, apparently catching his thumb behind the door knocker. Instantly all the other guards surrounded him and started to console him. One even kissed it better and told him it would be all right in a little bit. Ezra and Jrasta moved up beside the guard and Jrasta produced a surprisingly clean handkerchief with which he dabbed the guard's eyes. Ezra gave the guard an uncomfortably long hug, telling him it didn't look broken. Liam looked down to see Jep nuzzling up against the guard's leg, making soothing clucking sounds.

After far too long of a period of time, the Sergeant calmed down and took a deep breath. They appeared ready to move on again, but not before he glared at Liam as the only one who had not come to comfort him. He leaned in close and said, "I'll remember this!"

Liam started to stutter and realized he'd made a terrible mistake. "It's okay, Sergeant. I'm sorry you hurt your thumb."

"Too little, too late!" the guard yelled. "Do not act as if you care!"

He then turned from the prisoners, got down on his knees before the huge door and grabbed a dog's head near the floor. Turning it like a handle, a tiny section of the door opened outward, revealing a small passageway behind. He crawled into this hole and disappeared. Another two guards followed him and then one of the guards pushed Liam down to the floor and Liam followed the first three into the passageway.

The tunnel they entered was carved out of solid stone and went on for what seemed like an eternity. It was dark, and Liam couldn't see much of anything. Finally, a door opened up ahead, and he could see the guards crawl out. Liam followed a few moments later.

He squinted while his eyes adjusted and looked around the room. It was an elegant room with tables full of food and suits of armor along the outside walls. Off to the one side were two large doors with windows which led out to a balcony. The ceiling was domed at the top with curtains flowing through the room to add to its magnificence. There were servants here and there throughout the area who tended to the food on the tables and polished the armor. There were multiple normal sized doors (obviously the one they came in was for 'special' guests such as prisoners) and in the center of the one end of the room, at the top of a set of stairs, was a large and ornate empty throne.

The guards brought Liam and the others to the center of the room, not too far from the base of the stairs which led up to the throne.

"Kneel, prisoners! The Regent will see you soon!" the Sergeant bellowed.

Liam knelt along with Ezra and Jrasta. He tried to look out of the corner of his eye to see what Jep was doing and was surprised to see Jep down on one knee. Liam had never given much thought to chickens and their knees, but apparently kneeling wasn't a problem for Jep.

It was at this point that Ezra piped up. "Did you know that this young man with us is a traveler? He's from another world. In his world, he lives in the earth and is called a worm."

Liam shook his head, "Well, no, it's that the planet I'm from is called…"

"Silence!" Sergeant Dimmock screamed. "Tell me quick, is it true? You are a traveler?"

"Yah, I guess so."

"I said 'Be silent!'" he screamed.

By this time, all the guards were gathered around and clearly excited. "We haven't had a traveler in months! The Regent is going to be thrilled!"

The Sergeant stepped right up to Liam, pulled him to his feet and proudly said, "Welcome to our world. You have entered the land called, Snotworld. We are named this because of the great snot mines in the Booger Mountains not far from the capital city of Phlegm. The people of this land are called the Snots, although those of wealth and position are called Boogers, and the rest of us are called, Little Snots. There is a country to the south of us who are…"

Ezra spoke up again, "I told him all that. He knows all about Snotworld."

"You told him everything?" The Sergeant looked genuinely disappointed.

"Pretty much. Told him about the Hankys to the south of us and everything."

"You called them the Hankys?" The guards all started to chuckle a little bit.

Liam began to wonder if there was something else going on here of which he wasn't aware. The guards began to laugh harder and harder, and some of the servants in the room started to laugh as well.

By this time Ezra was on his side on the floor laughing along with Jrasta. Even Jep seemed to be nearly choking he was laughing so hard.

"Then I told him the Hankys were seeking to wipe out all the little snots!" With this, the last of the guards still on their feet collapsed on the ground. One of the guards started into a coughing fit from the laughter.

"Why are you all laughing?" Liam demanded. Something was up, and he was clearly being left out of the joke.

"Did you tell him about the waterfall?" one of the guards called out.

"Yah, and I said that the waterfall was The Great Runny Nose!" The Sergeant was weeping by this point and began to beg Ezra to stop.

"When I was done," Ezra explained between spasms of laughter, "I wiped my nose with my hand, and we shook."

At this point, all the guards stopped laughing along with Jrasta and Jep. They looked at Ezra with anger all over their faces. Even Jep had a seriously cross expression.

"You wiped your nose and then had him shake your hand?" one of the guards asked.

"Yah. I did," Ezra responded. He appeared a little a little less sure of himself.

"You crossed the line with that one," The Sergeant declared. Some of the guards began to reach for their swords.

"Hey, hey, it was just a joke." Ezra looked worried, and Jrasta and Jep each took a few steps away from him, trying to put as much distance as the chains would allow between them and him.

"That's just gross. If I wasn't wearing this uniform I would take you out back and teach you a lesson you'd never forget!" one of the servants declared, one hand on his hip and the other holding a broom quite menacingly.

"Why would we have this lesson out back? Can't we just sit down at one of the tables in this room and you can teach me what I need to learn?" Ezra seemed to miss the point on this one.

"You…" gaahh, "wiped your nose," hmmph, "and then shook his hand…" One of the guards struggled to get the words out. He looked green and heaved with the gag reflex. He was clearly trying hard not to see his lunch a second time.

"Enough!" The Sergeant commanded. "No more snot jokes! Young man, this world is not called Snotworld. That is a story we all made up to tell travelers because we thought it would be funny. Ezra, here, had to take it too far. This world is called Arestana, and we are the Arestanians."

"This world is called, 'Ara-stay-na?'" Liam asked, looking back at Ezra.

Jrasta spoke up at this point, "Liam! You're having trouble with normal words! First, you can't pronounce my name, now you can't pronounce the name of this world! What's wrong with you! It's pronounced 'air-eh-STAN-ah.' Arestana!"

The Sergeant stepped up again. "Enough of your oddness, traveler! The name of our world is simple. This world is called Arestana. We do not mine snot, in fact, we…"

At this moment, the Sergeant was interrupted. A man entered the room by himself and blew a trumpet. He then announced to everyone that he himself was the Regent. "I am the Regent, everyone! Regent, coming through."

The Regent wore a hat. He was, of course, wearing much more than a hat, but the hat was so large and so spectacularly designed that nothing else was really noticeable. The Regent tossed the trumpet aside to where a servant waited to catch it and strode forward.

The hat was about the size of a couch. Not a small, two-person couch which one might call a love seat, although Liam had never understood why that particular seat would be more loving than

41

a full sized couch. This hat was the width of a full sized couch and rounded up at the top so that at its peak it was likely taller than Liam. The hat had many different colors and appeared to be something in which the Regent could actually sleep inside if needed. If it was hollow, it could double as a tent for camping.

The Regent looked angry. "Why am I being disturbed!?" he hollered to no one in particular.

6. The Quest

The Regent walked up to the guards and then moved on to Liam and the others. He eyed the prisoners one at a time. He looked at Liam and seemed entirely unimpressed. He moved down the line to Ezra and had a similar response. When he came to Jrasta, he recognized him. "Hello, Jrasta."

"Hello, Ree-gee," Jrasta said, clearly trying to annoy the Regent.

"My title is 'Regent,' Jrasta, and you know it! Say it! SAY IT!!"

"Hello, Fleegent, sir," Jrasta responded.

"That's better, Jrasta. Carry on!"

Jrasta looked confused. Liam didn't know if the confusion was because the Regent didn't recognize his title was pronounced incorrectly or because Jrasta didn't know what he was supposed to carry on with, but he simply said, "Very good, your High-ney."

As he came to the end of the line, the Regent's face lit up. "Ahh, Jep! My good friend! What are you doing messed up with these three scoundrels? You should be staying in the castle with me!"

Liam swore Jep managed to portray both humility and dignity in the slightest tilt of his head to the Regent. The Regent leaned in close and let Jep latch onto his nose for a moment. Jep chomped down and then simply let go. Liam glared at Jep, mouthing the words, "Why don't you let go of my nose so quickly?" Somehow Jep smiled at Liam.

Sergeant Dimmock spoke up, interrupting Liam's glare at Jep. "Your Audaciousness, this one on the end is a traveler from a world where he is a worm."

"I'm not a worm, the world is called... oh, never mind." Liam was learning which battles were worth fighting and which ones were not. It was beginning to appear that few battles were worth the fight in this world.

"A traveler! Wonderful! We love travelers here! Welcome, my dear friend, to Snotworld. We are named this because of the great snot mines in the Booger Mountains not far from the capital city of Phlegm. The people of this land are called the Snots, and I am the Big Booger." The Regent stopped abruptly as he saw the Sergeant trying to get his attention.

"Your Odor-iferousness, he has already been told all that and, well, he knows that this is actually the land of Arestana."

"What??" The Regent seemed genuinely distraught. "How dare you tell him without giving me a chance to speak about Snotworld!" The Regent's voice turned into a whine, and he looked like he was about ready to cry. "You know how much I love telling that story!"

"I'm sorry, your Obtusiveness. I will be more careful in the future." The Sergeant didn't look sorry.

"That is enough! You will be punished! To the Rack with you!"

All the guards gasped with horror. Liam remembered something from school in history about the Rack being a torture device where someone would be tied up and stretched on a table. It didn't sound like much fun. Liam noticed Sergeant Dimmock did not appear concerned about this turn of events.

"Thank you, your Obliviousness. You are always so wise in your handing out of punishments." Dimmock looked a little annoyed. "This sounds like a most appropriate punishment for such an evil and rebellious deed. However, the Rack is quite a complicated machine. It requires a Rack Certification just to use it. The training for this is offered in a night school setting, but it requires three months, four evenings a week of training just to receive your certification. You, sir, were actually the one to institute this new certification."

"Silence! Enough of your talk of education and certification! Who in the castle is certified to use the Rack?" The Regent sounded annoyed but seemed distracted. Liam wondered if the reason the Sergeant did not look worried was because he regularly distracted the Regent with details about schooling and certifications and so forth. "Tell me! Who can we bring in to operate this Rack while you scream in pain and holler out your apologies to me for telling a traveler our world is not Snotworld?"

"Well, sir, that's the thing. There is only one person who is certified to run the Rack."

The Regent leaned forward and hollered, "Call this person to the throne room immediately so you may be punished!"

"Your Insensibleness, I am actually the only one who is certified to run the Rack."

"Then take another guard and teach them so they can torture you!" The Regent wasn't even trying at this point.

"Very good, sir. Consider it done." Sergeant Dimmock stood where he was and didn't move.

"I will then. Let that be a lesson to you. Do not tell future travelers that this is not Snotworld until I have had a chance to have some fun with them." The Regent turned his attention to Liam, appearing to forget all about the punishment.

The Regent stepped over to Liam. "Have you, young man, discerned what quest you have been given?"

"No, sir, I have not. I have just arrived in your… wonderful land." Liam thought he should try to be polite to a Regent.

"Well then, as the Regent of this wonderful land I will assign you your quest. It will be a dangerous quest. One which will take you from this land, across many lands. You will fight monsters and battle evil creatures. You will be tested beyond what you might imagine. But you will pursue a great treasure."

"Thank you, sir," Liam replied. "But sir, do you think you might have a different quest for me? One that's not quite so dangerous and which I may be able to finish, say, before dinner?" Liam was all for great adventures, but he preferred the kind he could watch in a movie theater while he ate popcorn.

"Silence! Once a quest has been given, it cannot be changed! You shall accept this challenge. You will travel beyond the Sandy Desert and retrieve the lost key to the magic box so that we might read the name contained in the box and identify the new king of Arestana. Years ago a thief made his way into the castle and stole this key. No one has ever seen him before, nor does anyone know what type of person or creature he might be. However, from information we have gleaned, we believe he is large, covered in scales, looks exactly like a dragon, breathes fire and responds to the name of Kenny the Dragon. He lives in a cave in the bottom of a great pit on the other side of the Sandy Desert. You will need to slay this person or this beast, whatever it might be, if you are to retrieve the key without dying. Aside from these details, we know nothing of this person or creature."

Liam didn't like the sound of this quest, but he was learning there was much in this world he did not like. He also was beginning to understand that there wasn't much he could do about it.

"If you, Traveler Liam, fail to complete this quest, do not feel troubled. We, as a nation, will grieve your death and the next traveler to arrive will be assigned this quest in the hopes that they will not fail miserably and die a gruesome death as the traveler before them has."

The Regent climbed the stairs and sat down on the throne. "To add to the wonder and privilege of this particular quest, I hereby declare that the one to return to this kingdom with the key will be appointed to the position of Royal Advisor to the Throne, a position of great esteem and honor."

At this, all the guards perked up and began to look interested. Sergeant Dimmock spoke up. "Your Obnoxiousness, I would like to volunteer to go on this quest as well. Not in partnership with the traveler, but in competition."

The Regent looked the Sergeant up and down. It was as if he had just noticed him for the first time and was not aware that the Sergeant should be in the dungeon torturing himself. "This is rare. It is not often that an Arestanian takes a quest in competition with a traveler. Rare, but not unheard of. I suppose that would be fine. Yes, you may go, and you may select your team to travel with you."

The Sergeant looked absolutely thrilled and nodded to the other guards. Each one, in turn, saluted the Regent before turning to follow Dimmock as he made his way to the door. All twelve wanted to take part in this quest. Liam had a sneaky suspicion that this would complicate matters somewhat.

"Now, as for the four of you, you are free to go on your quest. A traveler who may lead the quest. A young man full of desire for adventure. An old man with great skill and stinky feet (Liam wondered at that comment). And a chicken with great wisdom and insight to add great intelligence to this quest.

No one seemed surprised at anything the Regent said so Liam chalked the comment about Jep up to another one of Arestana's quirks. They each bowed one at a time to the Regent, starting with Jep and ending with Liam. With that, the Regent, along with the rest of the newly formed team, looked expectantly at Liam. Liam stared back for a moment, unsure what he was supposed to do. He then realized he was supposed to start the quest.

"Alright! Let's go, team." Liam felt awkward. He wasn't normally a leader. He looked down at the shackles he and the rest were still wearing. He wondered if he would end up being that one member of the team condemned to state the obvious when no one else could see it. "So, how do we get out of these chains? I assume we'll want to make this trip without them."

"Great idea, Quest Leader Liam!" Jrasta declared, his bare toes wiggling as he spoke. "You clearly have the leadership skills to identify the immediate objectives necessary to complete this quest!"

Ezra stepped up to explain. "It's easy. You see on the side of each of the shackles around the wrist there's a little knob. Just turn it, and the shackles will pop off."

Liam looked at his wrists. Sure enough, there was a little knob there. He grabbed hold of it and twisted it. He found the shackles did, in fact, pop off and they fell to the ground. "You mean we could have taken these off anytime? You don't need keys to open them?"

"Keys?" Jrasta asked, looking absolutely horrified. "If these needed keys, the guards would have to carry them which would be overly inconvenient for them! And think, what if they lost them! You'd be stuck in your shackles forever! It's the same for anything else: treasure chests, house locks, jails. If you needed a key for each thing that required a lock you'd have entire rings with keys on them! Best to make them so each person can unlock it without the need for a key. The only thing that needs a key is the magical box which holds the name of the next king."

Liam was about to tell them how dumb he thought this was and ask why they had not unlocked themselves earlier, but he noticed everyone had a look of shock on their faces. Even Jep was staring at him with a look that said, "You don't think these things through, do you?" He decided to move on. "Well, let's head out on our quest, I guess."

"That's the spirit!" Ezra cried! "Now, let's get some armor!"

7. Preppin' for the Questin'

The armory was huge. The room was dark, lit only by two lamps and some windows up near its ceiling. The walls were stone, and there was only one door into the place. The room was around the size of a small gym and shaped as an octagon. In the center of the room were racks loaded neatly with various weapons, entire suits of armor and a bin full of chain-mail shirts. Each of the eight walls was dedicated specifically to one item. There was a wall covered in various types of knives. There was a wall with swords of every type, style and size. There was a wall with just helmets. There was a wall with just breastplates. Everything in the armory shone like it was polished every day.

Liam stood there in shock. He had never seen anything like this before. He was also surprised to realize that the soldiers he had met might have had access to something like this. Especially considering how dirty, old and ugly their armor had been.

Ezra made straight for the swords, grabbing one in each hand and swinging them in a way that gave Liam the impression someone was going to die: maybe Ezra, maybe Liam. Maybe they would simply be having chicken for supper. Liam was sure of one thing, he needed to stay away from Ezra anytime his friend had a sword in his hand.

Upon seeing Ezra swing his swords, Jrasta spoke up. "All right, Ezra, put those away!" Ezra looked at Jrasta like he was crazy and then slowly turned back to the wall and put the swords away.

"Each of you, come with me." Jrasta led the way over to the bin full of chain-mail. He equipped each one with a leather shirt, putting chain-mail over top. The chain-mail actually went down below their waist and nearly to their knees. Jrasta then gave each of them what looked like a large shirt and a belt to cover the chain-mail.

Jrasta then led the group over to the wall of helmets and found one to fit each of them, followed by some armor for the legs and some sturdy boots. When they had finished suiting up, they looked quite impressive. Even Jep sported the armor quite well.

It was at this point that Ezra began to complain. "I wanted a full suit of armor! Like one of those over there!" He pointed at one of the suits and began pulling his new outfit off. Jrasta just watched as Ezra ran over to a suit of armor that looked as though it would fit him and began to put it on.

Ezra was quick to suit up and, in a matter of minutes, was lowering the helmet over his head. It was a good fit, and he looked quite dangerous.

Jrasta smiled to himself and called, "Hey Ezra, come on over here and let me show you something."

Ezra took one step and collapsed.

Jrasta collapsed as well but in laughter. After a few more seconds, Liam could hear Ezra gasping for air and crying out, "It's hot in here! So hot! Someone help me get this armor off!"

Jrasta and Liam wandered over and began pulling the armor off of Ezra. Jrasta grabbed Ezra by the shoulders and said, "Do you see why maybe we should go for something you can actually wear? The chain-mail is hot, and it does get heavy, but it's nothing like that armor. When you wear that armor, you can barely stand in here. Can you imagine trying to cross Arestana wearing that thing? Now, let's get you back into some proper armor and get each of you armed."

After dressing Ezra for the second time, Jrasta took the boys and the chicken over to the wall of swords and picked out a sword for each of the boys. Liam and Ezra each ended up with a two-handed sword, double-sided. They were heavy, but Jrasta promised they would develop the muscles to wield them. For Jep, Jrasta provided him with spears about his size which he could wield equally well in each wing. Jep went through some moves with the spears, and it was clear that he was no stranger to battle. Liam was gaining a new appreciation for him.

Liam bent down to adjust his boot and Jep came up and latched onto his nose again. This time it felt like he wanted to take the nose right off Liam's face and might have, if Jrasta hadn't pulled him away.

Jrasta then went to work on creating packs for each of the team members. There were packs for each of them to wear as well as a pack for them to put on their horse, which apparently they would be getting soon. He also found two knives for each of them, one for them to wear on their belt opposite their sword and another to place in their pack. Finally, he went into a side room and collected a number of odd looking sticks and strapped them to the back of his own pack.

"Alright, to the kitchens!" Jrasta announced.

Liam was all for this idea as he was getting quite hungry. He could tell from the way Jep was looking at his nose that he wasn't the only one.

They arrived at the kitchen to find a rather grumpy looking woman standing in the center of the room, directly in front of the pantry. On the other side of her, rows and rows of food and supplies could be seen. Jep, normally quite bold and willing to be right in the thick of things, seemed to hold back and refused to enter the kitchen. It was as if he knew a kitchen was no place for a chicken.

"Who are you and why are you in my kitchen!" The woman said, her voice just above a whisper. The quiet voice had a sinister sound to it, and her stare caused fear to grow in Liam's heart. Liam could see Ezra was shrinking back as well.

Jrasta, trying to keep his voice steady, spoke up. "We are here by permission of the Regent. This here is a traveler by the name of Liam, and we have come to get some supplies for the quest we have been given."

"What business is that of mine?" The woman asked, her voice rising in volume and pitch.

"It is not your business. We are here for some supplies, that's all. If you will step aside, we will take what we need and be off." Jrasta then turned to Ezra and whispered, "You know what to do." Ezra smiled and nodded.

"Everything in this kitchen is my business!" With that, the woman grabbed two pots, one in each hand and charged.

From the look on his face, Jrasta appeared completely unsurprised by this turn of events. He threw down his pack, pulled out two of the sticks he had fastened to his pack and charged at the woman. Using the sticks like swords, Jrasta attacked with a fury and speed which Liam would have thought was beyond Jrasta's ability. The sticks and pots flew back and forth, moving in a blur of motion as the two fought in the center of the kitchen, battling it out over who might gain access to the pantry.

Ezra grabbed Liam by the arm and said, "Let's go!"

Ezra bolted for the pantry, narrowly avoiding a stray swing of a pot and ran inside. Liam followed and, taking off their packs, they each began loading up supplies while Jrasta kept the Kitchen Lady busy.

"How much are we going to need?" Liam asked, not really sure what kinds of things to take or how much.

"We'll need a lot. We have a long journey. We won't need much water—at least at first. There will be rivers along the way. Grab food that will last a long time. Food like cheese, salted meats and some of those crackers up there will do just fine. Grab some fruit as well, and we will eat it first before it has time to go bad."

When they had nearly filled their packs, the sound of a great wail came from back in the kitchen. The Kitchen Lady had apparently spotted the boys in the pantry and realized what was happening. She renewed her attack on Jrasta with a ferocity that could only belong to a woman whose pantry was being cleaned out and Jrasta's face began to show the first signs of worry. This woman and her flying pots were clearly more than he expected.

The boys finished up and ran out, sneaking around the edge of the kitchen, away from the battle in the center of the room. They ran out the door, calling to Jrasta to let him know they were done. Jrasta began to back away from the woman, but she did not let up her attack. As she attacked, Liam started to notice the farther she moved from the pantry, the slower her attacks came. Jrasta must have seen this as well as he yelled out, "The pantry is the source of her power! Quick, someone close the door!"

Liam, bewildered by this turn of events, paused for a moment but decided this was no more shocking than anything else he'd experienced. He bolted back into the kitchen and to the pantry, grabbing the door with both hands and slamming it shut. He turned to see the woman slump to the ground, gasping for air and begging them to not leave her like this.

"Please. Please. I only ask for the right to live," The woman sobbed.

"Do you mean you'll die if the pantry door stays closed?" Liam asked, shocked and a little disturbed by how absurd this was.

"Yes. I can only live for a matter of minutes if my pantry is closed. Please… please…"

Jrasta looked at the woman and was clearly moved with pity. "Liam. Open it a crack. Just enough for her to survive."

Liam grabbed the handle and opened the door just a little bit. The smell of food inside crept out. It appeared to be reviving the woman, and Jrasta said, "You'll forgive us if we do not stick around while you recover. We must be off on our quest."

They bolted for the door as the woman climbed to her feet and began stumbling toward the pantry. They had only seconds before she would have the door wide open and be ready to resume her attack.

Heading down the halls, Jrasta told them they had one more stop to make. They needed horses. It was a good thing, too. With the chain mail he was wearing, the sword, the packs he was carrying and now the food in the packs, Liam was sure he could not travel very far on his own two feet.

They made their way down toward the gate they had entered upon coming to the castle. As they stepped out into the courtyard, the soldiers all turned and began to shout words of encouragement!

"It's the Traveler!" "Welcome, Traveler!" "Safe journeys on your quest, Traveler!" "Do not let Kenny the Dragon kill you, whatever kind of person or creature he might be!"

Liam thought he'd ask a really dumb question. "Hey, this might be a really dumb question, but if this creature we are going to fight looks like a dragon and has a name like, 'Kenny the Dragon,' do you think it's possible that maybe he is a dragon?"

All three of his companions stopped in their tracks and turned toward him with a look of incredulity on their faces. They all stared at him for a moment before breaking out in laughter. Jep laughed so hard he began to tear up and had to wipe his eyes with his wings. Jrasta collapsed in laughter on the ground and held his stomach while his toes wiggled extra fast. When Liam looked at Ezra, he was laughing so hard he couldn't breathe properly. One of the soldiers standing near had overheard and began a deep, slow chuckle.

When they had calmed down, Ezra was the first to find his voice and speak up. "Liam, I don't know what would make you ask that. Maybe you should think your questions through a bit more from this point on so you don't embarrass yourself." He put his hand on Liam's shoulder. "I'm just looking out for you."

Jep looked up at Liam and simply shook his head before walking on. Jrasta had a look of pity on his face. "It's okay, Liam. I think you've had a rough day with a lot of surprises. Perhaps in a couple days, if things settle down, you'll be able to think a little more clearly and ask fewer silly questions."

At this point, they arrived at the stables. Jrasta turned to the rest of the group. "We will need a few good horses. Jep can ride up with me. We'll ask the stable boy for his best horses with the greatest endurance so we can make good time each day.

They walked up to the stable boy. He was a young, thin lad, likely around seventeen. He sat there chewing on something that looked like a piece of grass as he stared at the wall on the other side of the courtyard. Jrasta stepped up and explained their situation. They were on a quest given by the Regent and needed some horses.

"Horses? I gots some horses! I gots big ones and I gots small ones. I also gots brown ones, black ones, white ones and I even gots some that are a bunch of different colors." The stable boy seemed well informed on what he had in stock. "How many horses you wants?"

"We would like three horses," Jrasta said.

The stable boy looked at Jrasta for a moment, then blinked, then stared some more. Jrasta seemed unsure how to proceed. He waited some more, but after a while, he seemed to grow impatient. He repeated his request, "We would like three horses."

The boy nodded slowly, giving the false impression that he understood the situation and was about to respond. They began to feel somewhat uncomfortable with the blank look on his face, and they realized that the stable boy had perhaps left them and gone somewhere else while his body remained glued to the spot.

"Okay, then we will just take three horses," Jrasta said to no one in particular.

They moved into the stable. Liam was getting more and more used to nothing in this world being what he expected it to be. He half expected the "horses" in the stables to be ostriches or even giant spiders. He didn't like the idea of riding a giant spider.

When he saw the horses were in fact horses, he felt relief wash over him. Jrasta went around and selected three good mounts for the group. Liam's horse was a dappled gray gelding that he named Lenny. Jrasta showed him how to saddle it and secure his pack just behind the saddle. Each one took enough oats for their horse.

Liam watched closely as Ezra and Jrasta climbed up into their saddles. He tried to copy what they did as best as he could, but he knew he still had a lot to learn about horses. He managed to get up on the horse, but almost slid off the other side onto the ground.

When they were all in the saddle and Jep was seated securely on what looked like a nest on the back of Jrasta's horse, they started out of the stable. Jrasta took the lead with Liam just behind so he could show Liam a thing or two about how to ride.

They passed the stable boy, and he looked up at them with a look of wonder on his face. "Hey, nice horses! I gots some horses! Some of my horses are just like those horses! I gots lots of different kinds of horses. You want some horses? I gots horses!" He then rolled over onto his back and stared at the cloudless sky.

The team rode on through the castle gate and down the street, heading for the gate of the city. Their quest was about to begin.

8. The Trail

The four of them made their way along the winding path which led away from the city. Liam looked back over his shoulder to see the city from a distance and was impressed. The entire city was surrounded by a wall with towers at each corner, plus another three positioned evenly along each wall. There were two gates on the wall facing Liam, and he could only assume there were two gates on each of the other three sides.

He stared back at the city and tried to take it all in. He had never before seen anything quite like it. As he stared over his shoulder, everything shifted, and he almost fell off of Lenny. He turned back quickly and grabbed hold of the saddle to steady himself.

"You need to keep your eyes on the road, at least till you get used to riding a horse!" Jrasta teased. As he spoke, his bare toes wiggled through the holes in his boots. "You're going to fall and hurt yourself!"

Ezra rode along with a big smile on his face. He appeared to enjoy seeing Liam struggle with his horse. He didn't seem to have any problem with the mare he was riding.

"Hold the reigns nice and tight and grip with your legs. No, put your feet in the stirrups and keep them there!" Jrasta was a good teacher, but not the most patient. He knew all the right things to point out but just expected Liam to pick everything up a little bit faster.

"Do they not have horses where you come from?" Ezra asked.

"Yah, but I live in a city, and in my world, we don't use horses in the city," Liam replied.

"Well, you'll have to learn here. We use horses any chance we get. We can cover a lot more ground on horseback than we can on foot. We can also carry so much more food and supplies," Ezra explained.

Since it was near the end of the day, they rode for only about an hour before they set up camp. Ezra made a fire while Jrasta built a simple shelter for them. Liam was used to camping. His family enjoyed the outdoors. Every summer they would pack up a tent and head out into the woods or the mountains. They would set up camp and enjoy the time together. The difference, though, was Liam had always slept in a tent that zipped up to keep out the bugs. This shelter had no sides, just a sheet held up by ropes and tied to the surrounding trees. It seemed more about keeping the rain off their heads than anything else.

They had a meal of some of the more perishable foods they had quickly collected earlier in the afternoon from the kitchen. Fruits and vegetables were on the menu. They had camped near a stream and were able to drink their fill and top up their water skins.

That night when they settled down and Liam crawled into his blankets, he immediately learned that he had never actually experienced living in the outdoors. The ground was like a rock under him. He could feel every bump, and the blankets simply weren't warm enough. When they camped back home, he always had a warm sleeping bag and a sleeping pad to soften the feel of the ground. A few minutes after they laid down, Jep started snoring and clucking in his sleep while Jrasta wheezed. He found it hard to fall asleep with such a racket, and his mind was swimming with the question, "How does a chicken snore?"

Then the bugs came. They came fast. They buzzed around his ears, bit any exposed skin and crawled all over him. They came in waves, attacking and eating. Some were small and crawled all over him. Others were large and would dive-bomb his cheeks and forehead.

He looked over at Ezra and saw that he struggled with the same problems. "Hey, you can't sleep either?" Liam asked Ezra. He spit a few bugs out of his mouth.

"No, I can't. It's kind of the bugs, the ground, the cold and the snoring that's keeping me awake. Aside from that, though, this is like sleeping in the castle. Comfortable and relaxing."

Liam smiled, despite how uncomfortable he was. Maybe he and Ezra would get along after all. "Have you ever gone on a quest before?"

"No, this is my first. You're actually the first traveler I've ever met. They come through all the time, but I've never met one. I've wanted to go on a quest for a long time, though. This is going to be a lot of fun."

Liam looked at Ezra. He was glad they were traveling together. "You're not scared of being eaten by a dragon or attacked by some strange monster?"

Ezra propped himself up on one elbow and looked at Liam. "I'm hoping that we get attacked by lots of monsters! That's what's going to make this quest so much fun! Sometimes people get boring quests like, hang up the laundry for the castle or give the servants some help down in marketing. One guy, a few years back, actually got a quest to design new hats for the Lords and Ladies across the land. He was, unfortunately, quite upset over this turn of events and actually designed the hat the Regent wears. Everyone makes fun of him, but he has to wear it because it's a quest hat."

By this time, Jrasta's wheezing had turned into an all-out snore. It was like Jep and Jrasta were singing a duet, a horrible duet.

Liam shook his head. "This quest thing is strange. So, we get this key and bring it back and open the chest. When they open it, there will be a little note inside that tells everyone who the next king will be?" Liam asked.

"Yep, that's exactly how it works," Ezra responded.

"Does the Regent want to be king?"

"Of course! Who wouldn't want to be king? The king has to do a little bit of work, but most of what he gets to do is sit around and have people feed him really tasty food. He gets to go where he wants, start wars or end them, go on adventures if he wants or not. The king gets to do whatever he feels like doing."

"If the Regent wants to be king, what will he do if his name isn't in there? Won't he get really mad? Do you think he might try to seize the throne?" Liam had been wondering this for a while. It seemed odd that the Regent would want the name of the king to come out and even more odd to think that he might simply give up his position of authority so easily.

"It would never happen! The people just won't follow anyone but the king. When the name is read, the Regent will step down, and the new king will immediately rule the land. He just gets to put the crown on his head, and away he goes!" It seemed to make perfect sense to Ezra so Liam figured it must be another thing about this planet.

"So, no one ever questions the king's right to rule?" Liam asked.

"No, of course not! Why would they?"

Liam couldn't wrap his mind around all this. He liked the idea that people didn't fight over who was in charge, but he didn't know what he thought about living under a king. It made him miss home even more.

Ezra yawned and put his head down. "But for now, we should get some sleep. Good night, Liam. I'm glad we can do this quest together."

"Good night, Ezra. I'm glad too."

Liam was cold and damp, and the bugs were terrible, but eventually, he fell asleep. He dozed off and dreamt that Harry was chasing him through a crowded street filled with horses and soldiers and peddlers, selling their wares. He ran for a bit and realized he was starting to not be afraid of Harry anymore. In his dream, he wasn't sure he knew why he was running. Maybe it was time to stop.

He woke up with a start. The sun was shining in his eyes as it crept over the horizon.

Jrasta and Jep were already up, making some breakfast. Liam glanced over at Ezra to see him pull himself out of his blankets. Liam got up and started to roll up his bed and stuff it back into his pack.

After breakfast, they hopped on the horses. Liam was a little sore after the short ride the night before and after his night on the hard ground, but it felt good to be on the road again.

They traveled in silence for quite a while, taking in the scenery and giving Liam a chance to get used to his horse. One of the first things Liam noticed, aside from the trouble he had controlling and staying on Lenny, was a growing pain. He kept getting cramps in his thighs and hips and the more they rode, the more his butt hurt. He knew when they stopped he would be in a lot of pain, and he feared that on the morning of the next day he'd have trouble walking.

He adjusted himself in the saddle a bit and noticed Ezra doing the same. Even though Ezra had spent a great deal of time on a horse over the years, sitting on one for a number of hours straight was obviously a new experience for him. Only Jrasta and Jep seemed comfortable with the transportation.

By mid-morning, they reached the top of a large hill and Liam looked back. From this height, he could still see the city off in the distance, but just barely. They had a lot of ground to cover over the coming days or weeks or months or years. He actually hadn't had a clear answer given as to how long this quest would take. When he would ask, he would get answers from Jrasta or Jep like, "It'll take as long as it'll take!" or "What's the rush?" or "Squawk!" The best he could figure from what he had pieced together was that they would be at least a week. He hoped his family didn't worry too much.

His thoughts were interrupted by Jrasta a moment later. "We'll break for lunch up ahead. There's a spring just on the other side of those rocks."

They came around the rocks, and it was just as Jrasta said. They hopped off their horses and Liam just about collapsed. Everything hurt, and he was exhausted. Over the last couple of days, his entire life had been turned upside down. Now he was on a different planet, traveling on horseback and sleeping on the ground. It was a lot to take in.

They had a lunch made up of some of their supply of fruits and vegetables, as well as some cheese. Liam worried they would get right back up on the horses right after lunch without a break, but Jrasta had another idea. "Alright, boys, stand up!"

Liam and Ezra got to their feet while Jrasta pulled out the sticks he had packed, the very ones he had used to fight off the kitchen lady. He handed one to each of them and kept one for himself. Liam saw that each had a handle on the one end. The sticks looked well-worn as though they'd been used to beat the side of a tree.

Ezra looked just as confused as Liam felt and asked, "Jrasta, what are we supposed to do with these?"

"They're practice swords. They're made of wood so that you don't cut off a hand or foot while learning how to fight."

Liam and Ezra both realized they were about to learn swordplay and both their faces lit up. This was going to be a lot of fun.

An hour later, neither Liam nor Ezra thought it was a lot of fun. Jrasta had taught them various moves, footwork and more. They had learned how to jab, thrust, parry and slash. He would stand across from the boys and, one at a time, practice a sword fight with them, and they would have to try to block his sword and attack. They never had a chance, and they were now covered with bruises from head to toe where Jrasta's practice sword had connected over and over.

Liam and Ezra had practiced with each other as well. Liam found not only could he get through Ezra's defenses without too much difficulty, Ezra could also get through his. Each boy was left with many bruises.

Liam wondered if any of this would come in handy against Harry, if he ever managed to get back home. In the past, the only way he could stand up to him was to try to talk his way out of the situation. He didn't want to use a sword on the poor guy, but he had a feeling the next time he met Harry, he wouldn't be scared of him.

At the end of an hour, Jrasta informed them they were done for the moment, and he put his practice sword away. Jep sat there, on a rock, where he'd been the entire time. If a chicken could laugh, he seemed to be doing just that.

The boys were about to strap their practice swords onto their packs when Jrasta told them to keep them out. "I can't practice anymore. It hurts too much, Jrasta." Liam rubbed his arms and shoulders and chest. He thought everything had hurt when he climbed down off his horse, but it was nothing compared with what he felt after an hour of swordplay.

"Listen! Not only are we after a key for the magic king box thing, but we are about to enter into some dangerous territory. You have to learn how to defend yourself and fight off an attacker. If you don't, you die. It's that simple. Now, do you want to keep practicing or not?"

The truth of this question settled in for each boy. This quest was going to be dangerous. They understood that if they practiced, they stood a better chance of survival. They each kept their practice sword out.

After they had loaded up their packs and horses, they climbed up again. Liam and Ezra both winced at the pain in their legs and backside. As the four of them set out, the boys found every move the horse made hurt them more. Liam hoped he would get used to riding a horse soon.

"Here's what I want you to do…" Jrasta began. "I'm going to show you a few swordplay techniques, and I want you to practice them over and over and over again. The key to fighting with a sword is to learn the techniques and moves so well that you don't even have to think about them. When someone thrusts the sword at your chest, you need to be able to parry and then attack. This needs to happen as a reflex. The more you practice, the longer you live."

Jrasta showed them a technique and then directed them to simply practice that move repeatedly while they rode. Now and then the older man would ride up to Liam or Ezra and adjust their moves a little bit or correct the way they turned their wrist. Something slight and something that seemed so unimportant, but Jrasta insisted it was necessary.

"Jrasta, where did you learn all this?" Liam asked.

"That's a story for another time, Liam. But I'll tell you this, I have fought in more battles than I remember and I have been on quite a few quests with quite a few travelers. You are not the first traveler I've taught how to fight with a sword. But enough about that, you're letting your shoulder slump too low. Keep it high! And

Ezra, keep the tip of your blade in the center, pointed at your opponent."

They rode on in this way for most of the afternoon. As the days passed, each lunchtime and supper, they would practice, and each day they would receive new bruises. By about the third day, Liam and Ezra both noticed there was the occasional thrust or jab from Jrasta that would not get through their defenses. They were learning, and their skills were growing.

Liam wondered how long they would have till they needed to use these skills in actual combat. He also wondered if the small amount he had learned so far would be enough to keep him and Ezra alive.

9. Booger Bullies

On the morning of the fifth day, Liam woke up feeling refreshed. This was the first time he'd woken up without feeling pain in just about every muscle in his body. He had slept well. He wasn't all that sore from riding, and he was getting used to the bruises from sword fighting. He was learning to see them as part of what he needed in order to survive. Liam and Ezra were also starting to notice their muscles becoming larger and harder as they developed their skill. They were both getting pretty good with the sword, and he and Ezra could battle it out for quite a while with neither of them able to get through the other's defenses.

Unfortunately, battling with Jrasta was a different story. He still managed to get through about half the time which meant if they were really in a battle against him, they wouldn't last more than a few seconds at most. Even so, they had improved much.

"You boys impress me," Jrasta said as they finished up breakfast. "I am pretty sure you are two of the best students I have ever had. You learn fast, and you keep at it. Good job."

Liam and Ezra both smiled. Jrasta didn't hand out a lot of encouragement and praise, but what he did say felt so good to hear.

"Thanks, Jrasta. That means a lot," Ezra replied.

Liam nodded his head in agreement. "Thanks for teaching us. You're a good teacher, Jrasta."

With that, Jrasta smiled a toothy grin back at the boys before forcing his mouth down into a frown. He growled something about how they needed to work harder and began to pack up for the day's ride. He didn't take compliments well.

As they were about to set out that morning, he told them to put away their practice swords and pull out their real swords. "Today you're going to practice with the real thing so you can start to get used to the feel of an actual sword. It's heavier, so it requires a bit more strength. Practice some of the techniques and moves you've mastered with the practice sword and make sure you do not lose your form or control."

They practiced with their real swords for the entire morning while on horseback. By the time they broke for lunch, both Liam and Ezra were exhausted again. The boys' shoulders ached, but they were excited about getting used to the feel of real steel.

As they sat down for lunch, Jrasta began to tell them what was ahead.

"Up till this point, we've had a pretty simple journey. The road has been fairly straight and flat, and there have been no thieves or monsters to worry about. The soldiers patrol this area regularly, and it's quite safe. But that is all about to change for us. Do you see the crest of the hill up ahead?"

Liam and Ezra looked ahead and saw a hill in their path. The road went right up the side of it and disappeared over the top.

"That is the edge of the area controlled by the King—or the Regent at the moment. Beyond that is where the danger lies. We will enter into the territory of the Lizard Men, we will travel through the Dark Jungle, move through the Sandy Desert and have to fight the guardians and more. Then, assuming we survive all that and also defeat Kenny the Dragon and get the key back, we still have to make our way back to Kings-Home. On top of all this, there are the Regent's Guards to deal with. They left just before we did and I believe they are just a short distance ahead of us. At some point, we are going to have to pass them in order to get the key before they do."

Liam and Ezra both sat there in silence. It was fun practicing with the swords and learning how to fight, but up till this point, it was all a matter of "if" they ran into danger. As they sat there, they began to realize that danger was just over the hill and neither of them felt prepared.

"What are we going to face first?" Liam asked.

"The first danger we will meet is the Booger Bullies. They are a race of people with huge noses. Their noses are so large, their nostrils are capable of fitting your entire head inside. When they attack, they shoot snot from their noses and slime you completely. Then, while you are slipping and sliding and gagging, they overwhelm you, take you back to their village and force you to eat of the Snot Root which grows in this land. The root causes your nose to grow and your body to produce a lot of snot. Eventually, you become a Booger Bully and begin attacking other unsuspecting travelers." Jrasta sat back and let that sink in a little bit.

Liam sat there for a moment and stared at Jrasta. "You don't actually expect me to believe that, do you?"

"What do you mean?" Jrasta looked shocked, and Jep rose from his seat and stared with indignation at Liam.

"I mean you told me that this world was called 'Snotworld' and that you mined snot and there were Booger Mountains and so on. It turned out that was all a joke to make fun of me. Now you're telling me there are monsters called the 'Booger Bullies' and I'm supposed to believe that? They shoot snot from their noses? This is just another prank you're pulling on me!"

Liam looked at Ezra, Jrasta and Jep. Each stared back at him, clearly not making any connection whatsoever to the Snotworld prank and this matter of Booger Bullies.

"Liam, I don't know what you think is odd about Booger Bullies, but I can assure you, this is no joke. The Booger bullies will take you and turn you into one of them. Of those who turn into a Booger Bully, few ever return." Jrasta shook his head as though Liam was speaking strange, unintelligible things.

"I've heard of them. They are the ones who captured the entire team from the last quest, and none of them returned," Ezra piped in.

"That's right. This is a serious issue, Liam. You need to be ready." Jrasta looked so serious, Liam started to wonder if this could be true.

"This is no joke? You're serious?" Liam asked.

"It's absolutely true. Now, as we cross that ridge, we need to put our real swords away and only use practice swords. These are not our enemies; they are simply enchanted by the magic of the Snot Root. We don't want to seriously hurt any of them in case they can be returned to their original state at some point." With that, Jrasta and Jep got up and began to pack up after lunch.

They hopped back up on their horses, skipping their usual lunchtime sword lessons. Each held their practice swords in their hands as they rode and Jep stood on his mini-saddle at the back of Jrasta's horse with a spear in each wing. He had a wild look in his eye as though he was ready to take down any threat. Liam wondered if Jep would still try to swallow a nose if the nose itself was bigger than he was. Only time would tell. That is, if the Booger Bullies were real.

They reached the crest of the hill in short order and came over the top. Liam wasn't sure what to expect, but the path ahead looked much the same as the path behind, it just appeared less used. As he looked far into the distance, he thought he saw the reflection of the sun off something metal moving along the path. He wondered if that was the armor of the 12 guards who were after the key as well.

As they traveled, Jep and Jrasta kept their eyes peeled for any movement. Liam and Ezra watched as well, but both felt so nervous they thought they might lose their lunch. Liam's hands were sweating so much he often had to wipe his palms on his shirt.

As Jrasta led them through the area, he started to point out signs which indicated they were getting close to Booger Bully territory. Liam almost threw up at the sight of the first one. On a tree, hanging from the limb was the largest, most slimy booger Liam had ever seen. This was saying something as Harry had some pretty large boogers which he often felt compelled to share with Liam at school. They stopped next to it while Jrasta went over to see. He examined it for a few moments before returning to his horse.

"This one is fresh. It's maybe less than an hour old. They are close. Be ready for anything, anytime." Jrasta was taking this all so seriously, and the boys could feel the tension building in the air.

By the time they stopped for supper, they were so far into Booger Bully territory that there were few trees or bushes around without some form of snot on them at various degrees of dryness. Liam and Ezra both found it a little hard to look around and keep their food down.

The boys felt tense and watched the trees and bushes closely for any movement. They ate in silence, fearful any noise might alert the enemy to their location.

As they finished their meal, Jep's head perked up, and his spears came out. Jrasta was instantly on his feet, his practice sword firmly in hand. Liam and Ezra jumped to their feet as well. Liam hadn't heard anything unusual, but Jep and Jrasta both had sharp ears.

When it began, Liam was instantly grateful for the hours and hours of sparring practice Jrasta had put them through. Instinct took over, and he was able to fight without having to think through each move.

About twenty Booger Bullies all came out of the forest at the same time, screaming and yelling. They didn't seem able to communicate all that well. They spoke as though they were really, really stuffed up. They were the height and size of normal men and women, but their noses were huge. Each nostril was clearly big enough for Liam's entire head to fit inside it, maybe his shoulders as well. He was not sure why he had compared the size of the nostril to the experience of fitting his head inside, but it seemed right. He hoped he would never have to find out for sure if his head could actually fit.

Liam and Ezra fought back to back, fending off the Booger Bullies' hands as they tried to grab them and drag them back to their village. At one point, they grabbed Ezra, and he hollered out for help. Jep was there in an instant, poking and jabbing with his spears. Liam was amazed to see that he did indeed still bite the noses of the Booger Bullies and saw the extra size didn't seem to slow him down at all.

Bit by bit, their attackers began to slink back into the forest, nursing their wounds from the wooden swords and looking mournfully back at the group of four. Things were looking like they might survive this attack until a nose blew in the distance and the Booger Bullies came back, attacking with renewed purpose.

Liam was already tired and about ready to fall over when about eight different Bullies came upon him. He jabbed and parried and thrust at each one, trying to injure them enough to convince them to back away, but it wasn't enough. More kept coming from the forest. He thought things couldn't get any worse, but he was wrong. It was at this point they brought out the big guns—the snot.

Snot began to fly, and the first glob hit Liam like a brick. He stumbled backward into Ezra and was shocked to find the snot was spreading all over him, moving up and down and around his whole body. It was causing him to have trouble standing. The mucus was slippery and gross. Very gross. He looked up just in time to see another one coming directly for his face.

He screamed, "Duck!" and dropped low to avoid catching this one in his mouth.

Ezra turned around quickly and yelled, "Where?" and the snot hit him right in his face. His mouth was, unfortunately, still open when it collided with his face and a surprising amount fit in.

He spit the snot out and gagged a little bit. "That was so gross!" Ezra cried, swinging his sword and taking down a Bully. He gagged again and then took down another one.

Liam and Ezra were both tiring, and the slimy snot was making it hard to keep their footing. Liam risked a glance over at Jrasta and Jep. The two them moved like lightning, but Liam could see they were about to be overwhelmed. Liam had an image in his mind of spending the rest of his life as a Booger Bully and felt terror and despair wash over him.

Just as they were about to be entirely overwhelmed, there was a new yell heard across the battlefield, and all the Booger Bullies took a step back, fear creeping across their faces. For a moment, the battle stopped as the yell sounded again. It sounded like a battle cry.

From the direction Liam and the others had come, a young woman appeared, a practice sword in each hand. She immediately began attacking the Booger Bullies. Some turned to run right away. Liam suspected the Booger Bullies had fought this new warrior before and weren't willing to repeat the experience. She moved with such grace and control that she appeared to be in the midst of a dance, rather than in battle. In seconds, most of the Booger Bullies were either unconscious or fleeing for their lives.

With the new arrival, Liam felt a surge of energy and attacked with more confidence. In very short order, the last of the Booger Bullies were fleeing into the forest.

The five stood there, breathing heavy and covered in snot. Liam and Ezra both slipped at the same time on the same large booger and landed on the ground in a pile.

Their new friend—if indeed she was a friend—stood there looking each of them up and down. She whistled off into the forest and from the way she had come, a beautiful solid black horse trotted up to her. She rubbed its nose and smiled up at it. Turning to Jrasta, she laughed and said, "You're slipping, old man! I've been following you since you left the King's territory. I wanted to see if you'd notice me."

"I was a little preoccupied with what was ahead of us, not what was behind," Jrasta growled, clearly trying to save face, but not doing a great job of it. Finally, he smiled at her. "It's good to see you, young lady. We appreciate your help. You came in the nick of time."

"You're welcome, Jrasta. It's good to see you, too. It's good to see you as well, Jep. I've missed you," the young woman said to the chicken. Jep inclined his head toward her and gave her a look as if to say, "It's good to see you as well."

It was at this point that Ezra crawled to his feet and walked over to the young woman. She was fairly clean with little to no snot on her, but after Ezra wrapped his arms around her and gave her a long hug, she was covered. He pulled away, and there were about a dozen lines of snot running between the two of them. She was nearly the same height as Liam and had dark brown hair with a green ribbon in it. She looked just about the same age as Liam and had a big smile on her face.

The young woman turned to Liam and introduced herself. "Hello, traveler, my name is DOHNK! I have heard of you from my grandma, Masha. She told me that you all might need my help."

"It's good to meet you, Dohnk. Thank you so much for your help. We couldn't have done this without you," Liam said, trying to be as polite and grateful as possible.

At the moment Liam said her name, all the others reacted and stepped back in horror. "What did you say to me?" DOHNK asked, gripping the handle of her sword tightly.

"I said, 'It's good to meet you, Dohnk. Thank you so much.'"

"How dare you! I come here to help you on your quest, and you call me a name like that!" She advanced on Liam. After having seen her in battle, he realized he was in for a real beating.

Jrasta came to his rescue. "Whoa! Hold on. He's new to this land. Maybe he just doesn't realize what he's said. Liam, why did you call her that name?"

"I, uh, thought that's what she said her name was." Liam looked at each of his friends in turn, and all of them had a look of disdain on their faces. Jep looked especially upset.

"I said my name was 'DOHNK,' not 'Dohnk!'"

Liam paused for a moment, thinking through what he had just heard. The names sounded exactly the same except she had yelled her name, and he had said it with a calm voice. "I'm sorry for how I said your name. It sounds a lot the same to me. Do I need to yell your name for it to be right?"

"If you don't yell my name, it is one of the greatest insults you can give someone. To call someone a 'Dohnk' is just... wow! That is so hurtful. You need to watch how you pronounce my name in the future!" DOHNK fingered the hilt of her sword while she explained this to Liam. He realized this was one matter of which he would need to be careful.

"Okay, DOHNK, I'll…" Liam paused for a moment. There was something about that green ribbon in her hair that didn't sit right with him. He put two and two together and realized what it was, but wasn't sure if he should tell her she had a large and disgusting booger up there. It seemed like it was slowly working its way through her whole head of hair. He decided since she seemed like an overly sensitive person, as evidenced by her anger over how to pronounce her name, he would simply let her figure this one out on her own. "I'll try to be careful with your name from now on."

"Well, let's get saddled up and back on the road," Jrasta commanded. "There isn't much light left, and I'd like to be out of Booger Bully territory before the sun sets."

10. Harv

The next morning they awoke to rain. It was just a light rain, and it didn't seem to be much of a bother.

They packed up camp, got out some breakfast, climbed on their horses and ate while they rode. By mid-morning, the light rain had turned into a waterfall. Liam and Ezra could barely see beyond the noses of their horses.

They stuck close to Jrasta who didn't seem overly bothered by the rain. Jep seemed to enjoy the downpour, and DOHNK used the opportunity to pretend she was swimming, doing a breaststroke at one point, doggy paddle at another.

By the time the group stopped for lunch, there didn't seem to be any part of Liam that wasn't soaked. He and Ezra were both feeling grumpy. The only nice thing was that it washed off the last traces of their encounter with the Booger Bullies.

"Do you think there's a way to avoid the rain?" Ezra asked after they climbed off their horses.

Jrasta had to holler back to him to make his voice heard above the sound of the downpour. "What do you have in mind? Go underground?"

"Is that possible?" Ezra asked, hopeful this meant there might be an underground passageway they could take.

"Not if you want to live. There's an underground river that flows through here, but we didn't bring a boat. At least I didn't pack one, did you?" Jrasta turned and went back to work, setting up a bit of a shelter so they could at least eat out of the rain.

In a few minutes, the four of them huddled in under the tiny shelter. Jep remained outside as he seemed to enjoy splashing around in the rain.

"What's the next bit of road look like?" Liam asked. "Any danger? I don't think we'd see it coming through this rain if there was."

Jrasta replied, "The next number of miles are pretty safe and easy, even with the rain. By supper, we should reach a friend of mine. He has a house, and we can dry off there and get a warm meal. He has a lot of space so we might be able to bunk at his place for the night. He's a little odd, though. He always tells me he's not my friend. That's strange since we've been friends for years. Every time I travel through the area I stop in there. He's such a joker, though. Sometimes he hides and tries to pretend he's not home. Sometimes he attacks me in my sleep. Other times I've caught him trying to poison my food. He really is a funny guy. You'll all like him." Jrasta sat back and seemed to go deep in thought, smiling to himself and apparently thinking of all the fun he'd had with this "friend" of his.

Liam looked at Ezra and DOHNK. Both seemed to be quite interested in going to this "friend" of Jrasta's to spend the night. Liam wanted to get out of the rain, for sure, but he didn't want to stay at a house where someone might try to kill him. How could he eat the food for fear that it had been poisoned? And why did no one see this as a problem?

They set out shortly after they finished eating. Everyone was looking forward to a warm house, and even Liam began to forget about things like poison and nighttime attacks and began to dream of a warm fire, dry clothes and a soft bed. By mid-afternoon, all he could think of was how much happier he would be at this friend's house.

As they neared supper time, the rain had eased off to a torrential downpour. He could finally start to see a little ways ahead, and it wasn't long before he could see a small house with smoke trailing up out of the chimney. The house was built of stone with windows on each side. The roof seemed to be made of grass. Liam had never seen a roof like that, even back in Kings-Home. He vaguely remembered something about this kind of roof being called "thatch." The front door was closed, and a light shone through one of the windows.

They arrived at the house and dismounted. Jrasta led them all to the stables out back where they unsaddled the horses, gave them some food and water and left them for the night. Heading around to the front, Jrasta knocked on the door.

From inside a voice was heard, saying, "Coming, coming!" The door opened, and a rather small, thin older man stood there.

"You again!" the old man hollered and tried to slam the door quickly. Jrasta put out his hand and easily pushed the door open wide while all of them walked in.

"Harv! It's great to see you, my friend! How long has it been?" Jrasta declared.

"My name's not Harv, and it hasn't been long enough. Who are you, and why do you keep coming to my house?" Harv tried to ask but was cut off by a big bear hug from Jrasta that lifted the little man right off the ground. Liam could hear Harv struggling to breathe and saw his arms and legs wiggling in the larger man's embrace.

"We need to take advantage of your wonderful hospitality once again, my friend. Our horses are already in the stable. We are all wet and in need of some dry clothes and some warm food." Jrasta gave the man another hug and smiled affectionately at him.

"Go away! You're not welcome here and if you don't leave..."

"Such a kidder, Harv! I always enjoy your sense of humor!" Jrasta interrupted. "Now, whose turn is it to make dinner? Harv always keeps the food in the back pantry."

DOHNK stepped up. When she arrived, she was put into the rotation for making meals, and this was her turn. "I'd love to make supper. I have a new recipe I'd like to try out!"

DOHNK went to work in the pantry while Jrasta went to a cupboard and found some dry clothes. He handed them out to everyone, and each went into a backroom and changed. After getting into the warm clothes, they laid out their traveling clothes by the fire and sat down to rest while DOHNK sang to herself in the kitchen. She had a beautiful voice. Very soft and soothing, or it would have been if she'd had any sense of rhythm and wasn't tone deaf. The sound was similar to a flock of crows being attacked by a bobcat in a garbage truck.

Liam looked over at Harv. He was chatting with Jep and Liam could make out little bits of what he was saying. "Jep, I just don't know why this man keeps coming back to my house. He comes, he eats my food, uses my clothes, sleeps in my bed. I just want to be alone. Who is he and why does he call me Harv?" Jep leaned in close and put a wing on Harv's shoulder as if to console the poor man.

After a short while, a delicious smell began to creep into the main room from the kitchen. It smelled amazing, and Liam's stomach started to growl.

"I think she's cooking the lamb I'd prepared earlier today," Harv continued with Jep. "I was saving that for some guests I was to

84

have tomorrow. Why does this man come here?" Jep put his other wing up on Harv's cheek, leaned in and latched onto his nose.

Before long, the meal was ready, and DOHNK called everyone to the table. She had prepared a beautiful supper, and they sat Jrasta at the head of the table. The table was large, but there were only five chairs, so Harv had to sit in the other room.

DOHNK spoke up, "Before we begin, I would like to thank Jrasta for leading us to this wonderful place of hospitality."

"Thanks, Jrasta," everyone said at once. A groan was heard from the other room.

Jrasta looked concerned. "Is Harv okay? Is he feeling ill? I guess we'd better not take any food to him. If he is ill, he probably just wants to be alone."

As they looked at the meal, they were impressed with how good it looked and smelled. Even the presentation seemed just perfect. It was laid out so well. Everyone's mouths started watering at once.

DOHNK spoke up before they could dive in. "I would also like to thank my grandma. She taught me everything I know about cooking."

Liam, sitting beside DOHNK, became concerned. "You don't mean 'everything,' do you? Because I remember when we had some soup at her house she…"

Liam felt a familiar grip on his tongue as his face was pulled down and slammed into the plate. Somehow DOHNK had managed to grab his tongue just like her grandma, and she was forcing him to eat with his face mashed into his plate. He could hear Ezra, sitting on the other side of DOHNK, struggling as well.

They feasted as the night wore on and by the end, there was no food left. Everyone felt wonderfully warm, dry and full.

When they got up and went into the sitting room, Harv was nowhere to be seen. A ladder led up to a loft, and they all used it to climb to the second floor. There were five beds up there, and one was already taken with Harv. He appeared to be trying to cry himself to sleep.

Jrasta did a quick count and realized they were one bed short. He moved over to Harv's bed and laughed. "You tease! Using that bed when you know that's the one I always sleep in. Hop up, funny guy!" Harv seemed unwilling to move, but Jrasta started pinching him and laughing till Harv climbed out of the covers and stood up. By the time he was up, the others had all chosen a bed. Turning back to his own bed, he saw Jrasta was in it and already snoring.

Jep had taken a bed as well, and Harv looked like he was wondering if he could share. Jep appeared able to read his mind on that one and simply shook his head, pulling out one of his tiny spears and slowly twirling it in his wing.

Harv went to the ladder to see if there was a place downstairs he could sleep.

Liam watched him climb down the ladder and felt guilty for taking one of the beds. It was soft, though, and he laid back. He rolled over and within seconds was sound asleep, dreaming of warm fires and good meals.

The next morning, Liam woke up feeling sore but rested. He looked around the room, and everyone else was waking up as well. Only Jrasta was not there.

"Probably harassing our unwilling host," Liam thought to himself. He wasn't sure what to do about all this. He thought maybe he should speak up in Harv's defense, but he knew he'd have no success convincing Jrasta anything was wrong. He realized the only help he could be was to try to hurry the group out the door to give Harv, or whatever his name was, back his home.

They climbed downstairs, and Ezra went to work on breakfast as it was his turn to make a meal. He went to the pantry only to return complaining that this was the last of the food in the house.

After breakfast, they all cleaned up and went outside. The sun was shining, the birds were chirping, but there was no sign of Jrasta. Harv was missing as well. They didn't want to waste valuable traveling time, but they were left with no choice but to wait and see what might happen.

After about an hour, Harv returned to the house, wearing a really big smile and whistling to himself. He had Jrasta's sword and knife in his hands.

"Here, I suppose these belong to you now," Harv said as he handed the weapons to Liam.

"What? Where's Jrasta? What did you do with him?" Liam asked the man.

Harv looked at Liam, chuckled to himself and said, "I handed him over to the Lizard Men. He keeps coming for visits, barging into my house, eating all my food and kicking me out of my bed. It was time I gave back to him. I described him to the Lizard Men last night, and it turns out they've been looking for him for years. We went for a walk early this morning over to the Lizard Men and, well, here we are! I could go for some breakfast!"

Liam was shocked and didn't know what to say. Ezra, fortunately, was never short on words: "You're too late, Harv! We finished up all the food in the house. No more breakfast!"

"Well, isn't that a rotten end to a very happy experience," Harv exclaimed.

11. Rescue Journey

Rescuing Jrasta from the Lizard Men was going to be a bit of a problem. For one thing, no one actually knew where they lived, and Harv seemed unwilling to point the way. For another, they weren't exactly sure how they were supposed to defeat an entire village of people called, "Lizard Men." Even DOHNK seemed a little worried, wondering if they had what it took to rescue their friend.

They began to pack all their supplies and get the horses loaded, being sure to pack up Jrasta's belongings as well. As they were doing so, Ezra piped up, "Did Jrasta have a map of the area? Maybe it points out the Lizard Men's village."

They rummaged through Jrasta's pack, finding a number of old and smelly items of clothing, along with many weapons. There was also a decent amount of food and supplies, the tent, his bedroll and a few odds and ends. They were about to give up, thinking Jrasta must have had it all in his head when they noticed a pocket sewn right into the side of the saddle. Looking inside, DOHNK let out a cheer. They had found a map.

They spread out the map on Harv's table and looked over the whole countryside. Harv didn't seem bothered by their presence anymore. It seemed as though once Jrasta was out of the picture, they could stay as long as they wanted.

In the very center of the map was Kings-Home with a little scribble next to it that read, "Good soup at Masha's place." Moving east from there, they could see the path they had followed from the city and through Booger Bully territory. The Dark Jungle was there as well as the Sandy Desert, and part way between Booger Bully Territory and the Dark Jungle was a little mark on the path. A note scribbled by the mark read, "Harv's Hotel." A little to the northeast of Harv's Hotel was another note with two words, "Lizard Men."

"So we head north," DOHNK said. "I hope we're ready for a fight. I have never faced the Lizard Men, but tales are told of their skill in battle and their ferocity toward trespassers."

Liam and Ezra looked at each other, both thinking the same thing. "This sounds dangerous, but if Jrasta is in danger, we have to do whatever it takes to rescue him."

They turned to leave and found Jep had already saddled Jrasta's horse. Liam thought of asking how a chicken, or rooster, could saddle a horse with nothing but tiny wings and a powerful nose biting beak but didn't want to be rude.

They climbed up on their horses and started east. At this point along the path, the land to the north was too hilly and rocky for their horses to make it through. They would need to find an easier path to use to find the Lizard Men. After doing a quick scout of the area, they found if they traveled east a little bit, they could leave the path and head north through a forest. Because of the closeness of the trees, they had to ride single file and often duck under low hanging branches, but the path forward was relatively clear. According to the map, they had about a three-hour ride to get to the village. This would leave them arriving shortly after lunch.

At around 11:14 am (according to DOHNK who claimed the ability to look at the sun and shadows and accurately tell time) the woods came to an end, and they entered a rocky area. They each had to hop down off their horses and lead them for fear their horses might stumble along the way. Liam's horse, Lenny, seemed to appreciate the break from carrying him.

Liam and Lenny were starting to get along quite well. When Liam first climbed up on Lenny, neither one was sure of the other. Lenny had been quite hard to control, and Liam constantly had to fight to stay in the saddle. By this time, nearly a week into the journey, both horse and rider felt comfortable with each other. Liam found he could stay on Lenny's back without difficulty and Lenny even seemed to try to help keep him in the saddle. Somewhere along the way, he had started thinking of Lenny as a friend.

As they walked beside each other, Liam looked over at his horse friend just in time to see Lenny stick out his tongue, turn toward Liam and lick him right in the eye. Liam did not enjoy that. He wondered if anyone in this entire world was normal. He didn't think so. He wanted to get Lenny back but realized the only way he could do this was to lick the horse in the eye. He believed he wouldn't enjoy that experience either, but Lenny might. Instead of seeking revenge, he just threw up on Lenny's face.

They walked on in silence till lunch time. Everyone wanted to push on to get to the Lizard Men's village as soon as possible in order to rescue Jrasta, but Jep looked at them all in such a way that they realized they needed food to keep up their strength in case there was a battle.

Jep scouted ahead a little bit and found a nice clear area where they could rest. Liam was on lunch duty today and managed to whip up a nice meal consisting of a hunk of cheese for everyone and some fairly stale pieces of bread. They ate in silence while Jep clucked at each of them in turn.

After lunch, they packed up. Their stomachs were unsettled as they thought about going into battle. Both Liam and Ezra looked ill, and DOHNK looked nervous.

As they set out, they found there were fewer rocks along the way. They were able to climb up on their horses and move at a faster pace. In a short while, they would be at their destination.

Not long after lunch, they began to hear faint noises in the distance and realized they were coming upon the village of the Lizard Men. Dismounting, they tied up the horses and scouted ahead. There was a hill before them, and as they came to the top, they crouched low. They looked over the crest of the hill upon the village of the Lizard Men.

At least Liam assumed they were the Lizard Men. They looked more like giant kittens, but they wandered about on two legs. Liam watched for a few minutes as he tried to make sense of what he saw. If they were cats, they would certainly look formidable. When they hissed and then let out their claws, they would be very dangerous. But these were kittens—human-sized kittens—but kittens just the same. Each one was absolutely adorable. There were long-haired kittens and short haired kittens. They were playing with giant balls of yarn and chasing each other. A lot of them were purring, and they had a giant statue in the center of the village of an elderly lady sitting in a rocker, knitting. About 8 of these human-sized kittens were sleeping on her lap, and Liam could hear their purring from where he was crouched.

With a lot of the things he saw in this world he just decided to ignore how wrong or absurd they were, but this was too much. He turned to Ezra and DOHNK and said, "So... one of you want to explain to me why the Lizard Men don't look like lizards, they look like cute kittens?"

DOHNK waived them back behind the hill and began to explain, but with a look of disdain on her face. "Liam, I would think it was obvious."

"No," Liam said, "I don't think it's as obvious as you think it is."

"When you heard that the Lizard Men had captured Jrasta, were you scared or were you excited?" DOHNK rolled her eyes as she spoke.

"I was scared, obviously. But back to the fact that these Lizard Men are actually Kitten Men..."

"That's the point! No one would be scared of a race of people called, 'The Kitten Men.' They would want to come and visit and maybe pet them and hug them! Imagine if we heard, 'Jrasta has been captured by the Kitten Men!' We would look forward to rescuing him. The Lizard Men, after trying out various names like, 'The Kitties,' 'The Pussycats,' 'The Cute Little Pets' and the 'Cutie-Pies,' realized that in order to strike fear in everyone's hearts by the very mention of their names, they had to choose a name which was actually scary. They changed the name of their people to 'The Lizard Men.' That way, when you hear about them, you are afraid! Come on, Liam! Think this through!" DOHNK waived them all back up to the crest of the hill to take another look.

As they looked over the village, they saw that there were a ring of large boxes around the outside of the village, presumably the homes of the Kitten Men... or Lizard Men. In the center of the ring of houses were a number of large structures. There was, of course, the knitting cat lady, but there was also a large pole covered in what looked like carpet. The pole was shredded, and chunks of carpet were strewn all around. There were also a number of large balls of yarn tied to a tree, and there was a large box, open at the top and filled with sand and the occasional large log or some such item.

In the very center of all this was a cage. In the cage was a thin older man. They had found Jrasta.

Liam wanted to run out right then and there and rescue him. He looked like he was in horrible shape. His clothes were torn, and he had tiny scratches all over his body. He looked very upset, like he wasn't too keen on being a prisoner of kitten-like Lizard Men.

Retreating back behind the hill again, they met to devise a plan.

"Okay Liam, this is your quest. It's time for you to lead us into battle." The way Ezra said it, it was clear there was no getting out of this one.

Liam collected his thoughts and started forming a plan in his mind. Leaning forward, he began to lay out for everyone how they would rescue Jrasta. As he spoke, he noticed Jep paying very close attention.

"Alright, we're going to wait for the cover of darkness and…" Jep gave him a look that was so intense he lost track of what he was saying. He pulled himself back together and considered what Jep was trying to say. He remembered that cats were nocturnal, they hunted at night. The rescue attempt would fail if they waited till darkness! He thought maybe suggesting dusk, but Jep seemed to suspect this and gave another look. "I mean we're going to go in mid-afternoon. Perhaps we'll catch most of them napping."

So far this seemed to be acceptable to Ezra and DOHNK. Jep appeared to be pleased and motioned for Liam to continue. "We're going to split up so we can attack from multiple sides." Jep turned his head just slightly, and Liam instantly knew that this was a poor plan. "Actually, we'll all go in together so we can watch each other's back."

"We're going to go in screaming and yelling and making as much noise as possible so that we can try to scare some of them." Again, Jep gave a look that seemed to say, "Liam, if you don't start thinking this through, I'm going to have to come over there and teach you a lesson. Now tell the troops that you are going to try to sneak in and avoid getting the Lizard Men's attention!"

"We're going to try to sneak in quietly," Liam explained. "If they're having a nap, maybe we can get in and out without being noticed." Liam seemed to think that Jep approved of this plan so far. Go mid-afternoon, stick together and sneak in. He only had one other idea and had no idea if it was a good one. "When we get to the center of the town, if any of the Lizard Men wake up, we'll all start barking like dogs."

There was a long pause after he explained this part of his plan. Ezra and DOHNK began to nod their heads, and it was clear they thought this was a good plan. Liam looked at Jep. The chicken looked back and lowered his beak just slightly as if to say, "Well done, Liam. I am impressed. I especially liked the part about the dog barking and why yes, I would like to bite your nose."

Liam appreciated Jep's encouragement but shook his head to let Jep know this wasn't a nose biting time. "Let's get back to the horses and make sure they're ready to ride in case we come out with a large group of angry Kittens hot on our tail."

"Kittens?" DOHNK asked. All three of them looked quite confused.

"Oh fine, I mean the Lizard Men!" Liam replied. "Never mind! It's time we attack."

12. Lizard Men

They found the horses just as they left them. Lenny snorted at Liam in a way Liam had come to recognize as affection. Liam rubbed Lenny's nose and fished an apple out of his pack. It was one of the ones they'd taken from Harv's place. Liam felt a little guilty about cleaning out all of Harv's food, but he had still taken about six apples to give to Lenny over the next couple of days. He couldn't get the whole "Harv" situation out of his head. Why was no one else seeing this as a problem?

They led the horses down the hill just a little ways. They didn't want to be too far from the village in case they had to run for it, but they wanted their horses to have a clear path ahead if they did come out in a rush. There were few trees and not many rocks in the direction they would need to go when leaving the Lizard Men village. It was also fairly flat and led roughly in the direction of the path on which they had been traveling, prior to meeting Harv.

Each one loosely tied up their horse. Everything was set so they could simply grab the reigns off of a tree branch, climb on up and ride away to freedom. This part of the plan seemed perfect.

They packed all the extra weight they would normally carry themselves onto the horses, keeping only armor and weapons. Liam felt an unfamiliar feeling in his gut. He had never gone into battle like this before. When the Booger Bullies had attacked, they weren't prepared for it. They simply had to fight for their lives. This time seemed different. They were choosing to go into battle. To add to this, none of them strapped on their practice swords but left them with the horses. This was a day for battle... this was a day for real battle.

Liam looked at Ezra and DOHNK, expecting to see confident faces, not worry or upset. Instead, he saw genuine fear in both their eyes. He began to realize that he was not the only one who was feeling tense. The only one who didn't seem nervous was Jep.

As Liam stood for a moment, considering Jep, he realized a couple things. He could see in Jep's eyes a great deal of experience and insight. He could see confidence in him, and he could sense that as Jep had survived many battles, Liam, Ezra and DOHNK could also survive. Jep's confidence and strength gave Liam and his friends confidence and strength. Liam realized they had a chance. They could do this!

As he looked over at Jep, he also realized something else. Jep wasn't going with them.

"Let's go!" Ezra said, starting to feel excited after Jep's enthusiastic pep stare.

"Jep's not going with us," Liam said. Ezra and DOHNK stopped in their tracks and looked at Jep.

"Is this true?" DOHNK asked, her voice a little less certain. "Is it because the Lizard Men look like kittens and, since you're a chicken, you don't want to go near them?"

Jep looked at DOHNK for a moment, and she understood. She leaned in close, and Jep gave her a little bite on the nose. Ezra leaned in as well, and Jep gave him a little bite on the nose as well. They seemed to all be having a moment with Jep. It was as if he was blessing them as they went to battle. Liam thought this was, like much in this world, a little odd, but approached Jep for his blessing. He leaned in close, and Jep latched onto Liam's nose with a chicken snarl. The pain was intense, and Liam thought his nose was about to be ripped right off his face. If it hadn't been for the Lizard Men village just a short distance away, he would have screamed out in pain.

"Help me, PLEASE!" he quietly begged the others. They came to his rescue and pried Jep's beak off his nose. Liam looked at Ezra and DOHNK, expecting to find shock and horror at Jep's actions, but found a look of jealousy instead. He could see that they resented Liam for Jep's attention toward him. Liam looked back at Jep and asked, "What's your problem? Why do you keep biting my nose?"

Jep looked Liam in the eye with a look which seemed to say, "Come here and I will tell you why I do this." Liam approached Jep. He was angry but wanted to understand why the chicken would attack his nose so viciously. As Liam came close, Jep inclined his head as if to say, "Many years ago I..." then, lunging forward, he grabbed Liam's nose again, biting down as hard as he could. Liam fell over backward and rolled on the ground. The pain he felt before was nothing like this. He quickly found a stick and in anger, swung the stick as hard as he could at Jep's body, hoping that maybe he could teach Jep a lesson so he would not attack again. Just as the stick was about to hit Jep, the chicken seemed to lose interest and let go. The stick, unfortunately, kept coming and slammed Liam in the face.

Liam stood up, refusing to talk to anyone or anything and stormed on toward the village.

It was mid-afternoon as they approached the village. They scanned the view before them. There were a few kittens, or Lizard Men, patrolling around the village, but most of the creatures were curled up in little balls. They lay here or there or on the old lady's lap. The few who were awake, however, seemed on the verge of falling asleep. There was much purring going on. Very few, at this point, played with the giant balls of yarn.

They made their way slowly down the hill, keeping to bushes or behind trees as much as possible. As they approached one of the large boxes around the edge of the village, they could hear a deep, fast rubble coming from inside the box. From what they could hear, there may have been five or six Lizard Men in there, purring away.

They rounded the corner and saw another three kittens sound asleep. Even though everyone else seemed happy to call them Lizard Men, they were clearly giant kittens. Liam decided he was going to call them kittens, at least in his own mind.

They tiptoed toward the three sleeping kittens, moving in the general direction of Jrasta's cage. The kittens before them were absolutely adorable. Liam didn't really like kittens, he was more of a dog person, but up close these kittens were so cute. He wanted so badly to pet one or give one a big hug. Apparently, DOHNK was thinking the same thing as she started moving toward a large gray kitten to her left, stretching her arms out for the embrace.

He grabbed her and was about to whisper to her not to fall for their feline charms when he realized that he didn't know how to say her name in whisper form. If he didn't yell the name, she would be very offended, and he was afraid she might actually hurt him. But if he yelled her name right now, he would wake up every kitten, and they would be surrounded within moments.

He wondered if he could pull it off by saying her name in a whisper, but with anger in his voice. "DOHNK, don't fall for their charms," he whispered. "If you wake this Lizard Man, he might wake the rest of the village."

He met DOHNK's eyes and the expression on her face told him he'd made another mistake, but this one wasn't making her angry. "Wow, Liam. That was the nicest thing anyone has ever said to me." A single tear formed in her left eye as she looked at Liam like she'd never looked at him before.

Liam had no idea what he'd said, nor did he wish to repeat it. The way DOHNK was looking at him was starting to make him feel uncomfortable. He turned to Ezra to find his friend staring at him as well. "Smooooooth, Liam. I didn't know you had a thing for DOHNK, but I don't think this is the time. Say her name like that again another time when we're not in danger. Let's get back to our mission."

"No, I didn't mean…"

"Shhh… focus, Liam," Ezra scolded, while DOHNK continued to look shyly at Liam. She even batted her eyelashes a little bit.

Liam decided to move on quickly from this one. It wasn't worth engaging on any of these points. These oddities were far too confusing for him.

They made their way around the sleeping kittens and crouched behind a small bush. Looking up ahead, they saw two more kitten-Lizard Men sitting on the grass, cleaning their paws. The creatures had a clear view of Jrasta's cage, and there was no way to get past them without being seen.

Liam scanned the area, looking for something he could use. Up ahead, there was a giant ball of yarn, not being played with by any of the kittens. But as he was considering how he could make use of this, DOHNK stood up and stepped out from behind the bush. Instantly the two kittens saw her and Liam knew they were about to alert the others. Before they could, however, DOHNK ran forward as fast as she was able and kicked the ball of yarn hard. Both kittens instantly forgot about any intruders and launched themselves after the yarn. DOHNK had kicked the ball so hard and so high they could see other kittens from other parts of the village moving after it as well.

This was their chance! Liam moved toward Jrasta's cage. Up close, Jrasta looked terrible. He was covered in tiny little scratches, and he smelled like kitty litter. Despite the scratches and the smell, he had a huge grin on his face.

He whispered to Liam, Ezra and DOHNK, "Do you see what Harv did to me? What a kidder! I mean, I didn't expect this kind of thing. He has such a great sense of humor! The next time we visit him, I think I'm going to make him an apple pie to say, 'Thanks for being such a good friend.' What a guy!" His toes wiggled very enthusiastically as he spoke.

"Jrasta, do you think maybe Harv doesn't feel the same way about you as you do about him?" Liam whispered to Jrasta through the bars. Jrasta responded with nothing more than a confused look.

Liam decided to ignore yet another strange part of this world and turned his attention to getting the whole group out of there. Sadly, he realized he had not considered one important matter. How were they to unlock the cage? Liam felt despair wash over him and felt foolish for not thinking things through. Had they come so far only to be held back by a simple lock on a cage? They wouldn't be able to break the lock without a lot of noise which would wake the kittens. But then again, even if he had thought of the lock, what would he have done? Their only hope was to take something solid and try to break open the cage.

Liam walked up to the cage and whispered quietly to Jrasta, "Jrasta, we've come to get you out of here. What we need to do is…"

Jrasta cut Liam off by reaching out, grabbing a handle on the outside of the cage, turning it and opening the cage door.

Liam looked on in shock. "Do you mean to tell me that you could have opened the cage at any moment? Why didn't you escape on your own?"

Jrasta looked horrified. "Open the cage door without their permission or without being rescued? That would be unheard of! I never! Liam, sometimes I think I'm beginning to understand how odd and strange you are, but then you come out with something like this! You need to consider people other than yourself!"

"There's no time for Liam's quirks! Let's get moving!" Ezra whispered to the group. "Jep has the horses ready to go, just the other side of that rise."

As they turned to leave, Ezra's foot kicked a small stone. Each of the four looked on in horror as the tiny rock bounced off to the side, directly toward one of the kittens. As it came close to the sleeping, human-sized feline, it hit another rock on the ground which launched it up into the air and right into the kitten's ear.

The kitten jumped up and made a sound kind of like a record scratch and hollered, "I'm being attacked by tiny rocks!"

All the other kittens jumped up, and the hair on their backs stood up. They hissed and puffed out their tails, but none of them were quite awake just yet.

They had precious few seconds to react. Liam grabbed both Ezra and DOHNK by the arm and made for the edge of the village. Jrasta followed behind, keeping up with the three of them. As they ran, the kittens were waking up more, and it wouldn't be long before they figured out what was going on.

Finally, one of the kittens announced, "Hey, isn't that our new litter box scooper? He's not in his cage!"

With that, all the kittens turned their attention to the group fleeing their village. "After them!" yelled a particularly cute little kitten in a soft, gentle voice.

By this point, the team had made it to the bottom of the hill and began to climb as fast as they could. Liam realized that sword fighting and riding a horse didn't help much when it came to running up the side of a hill. He started gasping for air before they reached the top. The horses were still a long ways off. Ezra was running just a little ahead of Liam, but he was struggling too.

They were nearing the horses, but the giant kittens were gaining on them. The felines were fast, and the distance didn't seem to be a problem for them. Liam risked a glance back and saw that there were about five kittens on their tail. "Keep running, they're just behind us!" he yelled. Jep was sitting on the back of Jrasta's horse, and all four horses were no longer tied up. Jep had gotten them ready to leave in a hurry.

Liam could see they would make it to the horses just in time, but that wouldn't leave them enough time to climb into the saddle and get the horses moving. They needed a distraction.

All the others were just ahead of him. He knew what he needed to do.

Bringing himself to a stop, he turned around and drew his sword. He didn't think he could take on all five of the kittens— Lizard Men—by himself, but he had to try. The kittens saw him stop and turned their attention to him. All five came straight at him, and he could see from the feral looks on their faces, he was not likely to make it out of this one alive.

He felt a wave of calm come over him. He wasn't worried. He would take this stand for his team, and he would give himself up for them. They had been through so much together, and he knew they were worth the sacrifice to him. He would do what he could to earn their freedom. As the kitten/Lizard Men came close and were just about upon him, he drew his knife in his left hand, ready to fight to the death for those he loved.

Liam saw a flash of movement in the corner of his eye and Jep ran in front of him. He stood between Liam and the charging beasts. Jep opened his mouth, and for a second, Liam thought he was preparing to bite their noses, but then Jep let out the loudest, meanest sounding bark he had ever heard. He then let out another, and another. He sounded like a vicious guard dog. If it hadn't been for the danger of the Lizard Men, it would have been quite funny watching a chicken bark like a Doberman.

The Lizard Men, however, did not think it was funny. The charging horde of kitten-like Lizard Men ground to a halt only a short distance from Jep. Their fur stood up, their tails puffed out and their backs arched. They hissed at Jep. They seemed unsure whether they should be afraid of Jep or eat him. The barking continued, and Jep added the odd growl into the mix. This was clearly too much for the Lizard Men. One by one, they turned and ran, till only a single Lizard Man stood before Jep. He hacked and coughed up a fur ball before he too turned and ran.

Jep moved over and started kicking at the present left by the last Lizard Man while the rest of the group left the horses and came back. "Wow! That took some real courage, Jep," Jrasta said.

"It sure did, Jep! You were amazing!" Ezra exclaimed.

"The rest of us were just running away like cowards, especially Liam, but you ran right at the danger. I can't believe you were willing to risk yourself for us, Jep!" DOHNK said to the chicken.

"Hey, I stopped to fight them off..." Liam started, but Jep gave him a look. He knew Jep would not take kindly to Liam stealing the spotlight. "But I guess in the end, you were the one who saved the day, Jep."

Jep held his head high and walked proudly back to the horses. He hopped up onto the back of Jrasta's horse and sat down, ready to ride.

"This is why we need Jep along. We wouldn't last two minutes out here without him," Jrasta declared. "No one else would even think of putting themselves in danger to save the rest of the group."

Liam shook his head as he climbed into the saddle.

13. The Aron Mountains

The five companions made their way through the trees. It had been hours since Liam had nearly sacrificed himself to fight off the Lizard Men and been saved from certain glory by Jep. Liam wasn't sure if he was relieved that he hadn't needed to fight off the giant kittens or if he was upset that Jep had received all the credit while Liam was entirely overlooked.

The way forward wasn't quite as smooth traveling as the way to the Lizard Men Village. There were many hills and rocks to climb over or around, but Jrasta explained they would save time by moving cross country. The way they had come would have been the easiest route, but from the village, they could move east for a time till they reached the foothills of the Aron Mountains then head southeast across the Aron Plains toward the path. This would, according to Jrasta, be quite a difficult journey, but would save about a day's travel. They had already lost a significant amount of time, and the Regent's Guards had had a head start.

For a time it was slow going as they entered a forest of pine trees. The branches hung low, and the trees grew close together. Finding a way through proved difficult. Jrasta pushed them on till evening, and they made their way to the far side of the forest. They set up camp in a clearing with the pine forest to the West of them and the Aron Mountains up ahead.

Liam built the fire that evening, and the meal was simple: cheese and bread they had pilfered from poor Harv's house. They ate in silence, thinking over the day's events.

Finally, Liam spoke up. He knew he should let the whole "Harv thing" go. He also knew it was a waste of time to try to convince Jrasta that Harv didn't see him as a friend. This whole mess, however, was bothering Liam so much he had to at least try.

"So, Jrasta, I bet it was a surprise when Harv turned you over to the Lizard Men. It has to be hard to realize someone you thought was your friend could betray you like that and end up not caring about you at all."

Jrasta stopped chewing on his stale bread and dry cheese for a moment, then swallowed what was in his mouth. He looked thoughtfully at Liam for a moment before replying. "Liam, sometimes you say the strangest things. I wonder if perhaps your world might be a little different than ours. I get the impression you find certain things here strange. Perhaps I would find some things strange in your world."

Liam nodded, and Jrasta continued. "Let me tell you about Harv. I met Harv when I was about ten years old. We instantly became fast friends. His dad was a carpenter, and he was trying to learn the craft. He would work day and night on a chair, making sure it was perfect. I would come over and sit on it and jump on it to see if it could hold my weight and most times it would break eventually. If not at first, I could find a way. He would then weep and say something about spending day and night working on that or some other such nonsense. He was always such a joker."

"Eventually, he gave up on such a foolhardy, 'I wanna be a carpenter like my dad when I grow up' plan. I mean, who learns a craft like carpentry and tries to do it well? Instead, he tried moving to another city. He said something about how he needed to get away. I tracked him down and found him in the new city. He was trying his hand as a soldier. I would take his armor and leave it out in the rain so it would rust. I would hide his sword. I told him how a short little guy like him could never succeed as a guard or soldier. Eventually, he gave up this foolish dream as well. He then moved on to another city and another. I would always track him down and see what he was up to."

"Liam, maybe all this seems strange to you, but I would do this because that's what friends do. Occasionally after I would find him in a city, he would call in guards and ask them to help me move out. Maybe that seems strange to you as well, but that's also what friends do. They help each other!"

"As time wore on, he obviously started to notice that I was very thin-skinned. Insults and hurtful words were hard for me to hear and I didn't respond well to them. So when I showed up, he would start to insult me and tell me to go away. At first, I wondered if he really wanted me to go away, but then I realized this was the greatest proof of his friendship toward me. He was trying to teach me how to respond when someone insulted me. Sometimes I would find he would make some soup for me and he would slip some poison in. I was always very grateful for those times. If it wasn't for that, I would not have learned to test each meal ahead of time to make sure it was safe to eat. Who knows how many times I would have been taken by surprise and maybe even died by poison from someone who didn't care for me as Harv does! Harv has taught me many things."

"When he moved out to the house along the path, near the Lizard Men, he didn't tell me where he was moving. He just suddenly disappeared. I had to search for months for him, and when I finally found him, the look on his face was wonderful. He was so surprised. I guess he didn't expect me to find him so quickly, but I have learned to be such a good tracker because of Harv and his frequent moves."

"I'm not sure yet what Harv was trying to teach me when he handed me over to the Lizard Men. He was probably just trying to keep me on my toes. But you see, Liam, Harv has always been such a good friend to me. Perhaps in your world, friends express their love and concern differently, but this is how Harv and I show each other our love for one another as close friends."

As Jrasta shared this story of his 'friendship' with Harv, Liam looked on in wonder. He wasn't really sure what to say in response. He wanted to argue with Jrasta and help him to see that Harv didn't seem quite as interested in this friendship as Jrasta. He wanted to help him see that Harv was actually a danger to him, but he realized Jrasta seemed to enjoy the friendship and the danger. The biggest issue, however, was Liam felt bad for poor Harv! There didn't seem any way to convince Jrasta to leave that poor man alone.

"But enough about my good friend Harv!" Jrasta declared, standing up. "There's still a little bit of light left. Grab your practice swords, everyone. No real swords today. Let's get some training in!"

After having traveled for so many days and having practiced just about every night, Liam's muscles were no longer sore. He was noticing some new muscle developing and finding it took a lot of practice before he would get tired. When he had first started on this quest, practice times were fun but exhausting. In those early days, he had wondered how he could survive in a sword fight if it lasted more than a couple minutes. The exhaustion would set in, and he would be gasping for air in no time. By this point, he was practicing longer without getting tired, and he was always disappointed when sparring ended.

He and Ezra were also getting better by the day. Neither were as good as Jrasta or DOHNK, but it was clear the boys were improving.

Tonight, however, Jrasta announced they were going to learn something new. Liam and DOHNK paired up, and Jrasta and Ezra paired up. The goal was for Liam and Ezra to learn how to disarm their opponents and keep their opponents from disarming them.

Within seconds, Liam's sword was on the ground. DOHNK seemed to have a way of simply knocking the sword out of his hand or striking the fingers hard enough that he lost his grip on the handle. Ezra didn't seem to be doing any better as Liam looked over to see Ezra's sword on the ground and his friend rubbing his hand.

As the sun began to set, Jrasta and DOHNK each taught them how to hold their sword to keep it from being knocked out of their hands and how to disarm their opponent. They were quick learners, and in short order, they could hold on to their swords and even occasionally disarm DOHNK or Jrasta!

When the sun set, they put their swords away and settled down for the night. Ezra looked over at Liam, and both were proud of what they had learned.

The next morning, they were awakened by a cold wind blowing down from the mountains. They got up quickly and scarfed down some breakfast before packing up. They had learned how to pack up in minutes and were on their horses in a short amount of time, heading east toward the Aron Mountains. The Mountains were huge, and the peaks were all hidden in the clouds. Liam remembered how Ezra had mentioned princesses living up on top of mountains. He wondered if it was true and how they could survive up there.

The way ahead was fairly easy traveling as the forest was behind them. The ground leading away from the forest was grassy with only a few large rocks scattered here and there. By mid-afternoon, they had reached the foothills of the Aron Mountains and turned southeast toward the path. That evening, they camped by a river flowing down out of the mountains.

Liam and Ezra both had a real problem. They stunk. In fact, maybe it was his imagination, but it seemed to Liam that whenever they stood too close to anything growing, like a bush or a flower or a tree, the leaves or petals would start to wilt... just a little bit. Even Jep appeared less willing to bite Liam's nose, which seemed like a plus to Liam, but the stink was getting pretty bad. That afternoon, Ezra had raised his arm to point at a really odd looking tree growing on the side of a rock, and the smell had hit Liam like a truck, knocking him clean off his horse. When Ezra came to check on Liam to see if he was okay, he crouched down next to his friend and Liam's smell caused Ezra to gag.

It was time to deal with this problem. Jrasta, who certainly didn't have a pleasant aroma himself, ordered Liam and Ezra to go take a bath in the river.

The river was ice cold. In fact, it seemed to Liam that it was colder than ice. He wasn't sure that he could submerge himself in it without freezing to death. He wondered if the stink would freeze on him and he could chip off the frozen stink chunks.

They left the group and traveled a little way upstream for privacy. Both stripped down to their shorts and came to the edge of the river. Neither wanted to get in as even the rocks seemed to be shivering, but they knew what they had to do. Liam put his hand on Ezra's shoulder in order to encourage him and was about to say, "We can do this. Let's just wash up and be done with it," but in raising his arm, the stink from the armpit was released, and both boys screamed out in agony. The smell was too much. They covered their noses and stumbled around, but in their panic to block the stink, Liam tripped and landed on Ezra, causing them both to roll right into the river.

The experience of hitting the water was similar to boxing. When you enter a boxing ring with someone who is eighteen times

112

your size with arms the size of tree trunks, you know you are going to hurt. Then, when your opponent hits you with all he's got, your whole body screams out in agony, and your brain asks you quite clearly, "Why? What have I done to you? All I do is sit around and pretend I don't exist and this is how you repay me?"

Both boys sucked in their breath when they hit the water. In seconds, they found they were trying to suck in more air, but their lungs were full. The bottom of the river might have been down there, but neither boy could feel their feet anymore.

They desperately began to wash themselves off, finding even the water didn't want any part of what was going on in their armpits. It was as if the water was jumping out of their hands as it came close to the pits, but in time they managed to get themselves washed. Looking down river, they could almost see a stream of dirt and stink flowing away from them, and the river seemed to be writhing in agony from the grossness of it.

After about sixty agonizing seconds, they climbed out of the river smelling much better. They shivered together and wept as they longed for warmth. They dried themselves off and chipped off what ice had formed in their hair and fingers before pulling on the rest of their clothes and heading back to the campsite.

When they arrived, they found a warm fire waiting for them and Jrasta had put together a nice meal of something Liam couldn't recognize. After supper, they practiced their sword-fighting till the sun set. The movement and activity helped after such cold water. They headed to bed smelling much better and feeling quite relaxed.

14. Mary

After setting out the next morning, they found the path to be more difficult. They first had to cross the freezing cold river in which they had bathed the evening before. The horses didn't seem to like the cold any more than Liam and Ezra. Both boys noticed the grass and plant life close to the river all looked somewhat dead this morning flowing downstream from where they had bathed the night before. It was a reminder to them not to let the stink get so bad again.

The landscape after the river was very rocky and quite hilly. They had to climb down off their mounts now and then to lead the horses through rough terrain. The cold wind blowing off the mountains seemed to grow worse as the day wore on and they were grateful for the extra layers of clothing they had in their packs.

By mid-morning, they crested a hill and could see far across the land. Jrasta said they should reach the path again by lunchtime and that the shortcut through the foothills would have saved them a decent amount of traveling.

It was at this point that DOHNK pointed off into the distance. "There are some soldiers down there!"

Jrasta looked back in the direction DOHNK had been pointing. The path wound back toward Harv's house and the city of Kings-Home. At first, Liam couldn't see anything unusual, but sure enough, a short distance back was a group of soldiers making their way along the path.

"It's the Regent's guards. If we hurry, we can get to the path and be a little ahead of them," Jrasta said to the group.

They urged their horses on. The terrain ahead was smooth, and they were able to move at a good steady pace. Liam was grateful for the time he had spent on Lenny. He didn't fall off quite so often anymore. When they had first set out, moving at a trot or gallop was nearly enough to throw Liam off Lenny's back, but by this point in the journey, it was easy. Unfortunately, his butt still hurt from being in the saddle every day.

They arrived at the path and turned east. They kept up a fast pace, but as they looked back, the guards appeared to have picked up their pace as well. Up till this point, the guards likely thought they were ahead of Liam and Ezra and their group, but losing the lead seemed to give them the push they needed to drive hard.

"Why do we need to stay ahead of the guards? Why don't we just let them get the key?" Liam asked, after riding hard for about an hour, but not finding the distance between them and the guards getting any greater.

"Why are you here, Liam? Is it to ride a horse or complete a quest?" Jrasta asked.

"To complete a quest, of course!" Liam said. He wondered what that had to do with anything.

"Here's the situation. I've seen this happen before, Liam. You want to get home, right? The only way you can get home is if you complete your quest. But the Regent told the guards that if they complete the quest, they'll be advisors to the throne. That's a pretty sweet gig. You get to sit around all day, tell the king what you think he should do, you get paid well, and since the king doesn't make decisions on weekends or from September to February, you get a lot of time off. The guards all want to be advisors to the throne. They're going to try to finish the quest themselves and get that promotion. If they complete the quest, though, YOU won't have completed it, and YOU won't get to go home. This has happened before to travelers. Sometimes they manage to get another quest, but most of the time they get one chance, and if they miss it, then they are stuck here forever."

"I see," Liam said, more to himself than anyone. He hadn't realized that this could be his only chance to get home. It made him start to miss his family and school and even Harry... a little. Maybe not Harry so much, but he'd be willing to put up with Harry if it meant he could go home again.

They pushed on all afternoon and into the evening, but in time the horses started to slow down. Jep flapped his wings to get everyone's attention. He looked at them with his head slightly cocked to one side as if to say, "We're going to have to stop to give the horses a rest. It'll do us no good if we run the horses too hard and they collapse from exhaustion!"

No one wanted to stop, but as they looked back, the guards seemed to have come to a halt as well. It was time to give Lenny and the other horses a rest.

They dismounted. Each of them, aside from Jep, seemed to be sore and ready to head to bed. They made a fire, had a quick supper and pulled out their practice swords.

"These guards aren't playing around," Jrasta explained. "We may need to fight them tomorrow if they catch up with us. For now, both the guards and the five of us need a rest so we should be okay for the night. We will need to be prepared for a fight tomorrow, so this evening we will practice with real swords. Try not to cut each other up!"

They each practiced till sunset and then crawled into their blankets. Jrasta said they needed to keep an eye out this night and volunteered to take the first watch. Liam and Ezra dozed off almost immediately.

In what seemed like minutes, DOHNK was waking Liam up. "Your turn, sleepy-head. You have to take the last watch. Keep an eye out. Wake us up if you see anything out of the ordinary and when you see it start to get light in the East, get us up so we can get moving early. We need to be on the road before sunrise today."

With that, DOHNK simply collapsed on the ground and fell asleep where she landed. Liam took his blanket and spread it over her to keep her warm.

He had never taken a "watch" before. He wasn't entirely sure what he was supposed to do or how he was supposed to stay awake. He also didn't know what he should be looking for. DOHNK had said to wake everyone if he saw anything out of the ordinary. There was very little in this world that seemed ordinary to him.

After about fifteen minutes of nothing, just slapping himself in the face to stay awake, he was quite bored. It was cold, dark and lonely. There was no movement. There was nothing.

There was nothing, that is, till he heard a growl and a loud scraping noise. Something was on the road ahead. It was coming from the east, the direction they were heading. It couldn't be the soldiers as they were behind them and he assumed none of the soldiers could growl like that. He began to be able to make out a shape. This thing, whatever it was, appeared to be about the height of two elephants, one on top of another. It was moving slowly and dragging a large round something behind it. Liam wasn't sure what to do. He wondered if he should wake everyone, but thought he'd go over and take a look first. He moved toward the creature to scout it out before waking up his friends.

As he drew close, he was horrified to see that it was some kind of giant beast. It had scaly, gray skin, kind of like a fish, but the scales seemed harder and more like armor on its body. It really was about as tall as two elephants, one on top of another, but the creature was wide as well. It walked on two legs which were as big around as an old oak tree, and its arms were so muscular Liam thought there wouldn't be much it couldn't pick up and throw. It had claws on each foot and hand. Each claw was about as long as a baseball bat, and with its jaws and teeth, it looked like it could bite through solid steel.

The most terrifying part, however, was what the beast dragged behind itself as it walked. It was a giant net full of people! None of them were moving. They were just crammed in the net, one on top of another. Arms and legs were hanging out the holes in the net, but none of the holes were large enough for anyone to escape. The creature looked like it had collected about fifty people. Liam was terrified both of what would happen to those people and about the idea of being caught in there himself!

Liam looked on in horror as the creature passed him and then stopped. It slowly turned its head and looked right at the camp. When it saw the campfire, it turned and started making its way toward his sleeping friends.

Liam's only hope was in how slowly this creature moved. Perhaps he could save his friends if he could wake them up quickly. "Wake up! Wake up! We're under attack! Wake up!" he yelled, as he ran toward the campsite.

The creature, taking notice of him for the first time, looked down and slowly reached for him. Liam dodged the creature, drew his sword and took a swing at the beast's arm. Just as he feared, the creature's scales were like armor, and his sword just bounced right off.

"Wake up!" he screamed again.

This time, everyone heard him and grabbed their swords. They jumped to their feet, ready to defend themselves and began running out toward the dark shape approaching their campsite.

"Remember your training!" Jrasta hollered out to everyone. "Form up and get ready to defend!"

They spread out, and Liam took his place beside Ezra. The creature continued to approach, dragging the net of people behind.

"Be ready, everyone! Whatever this beast is, we have to stand firm! Protect one another and fight bravely!" Jrasta said to everyone. "This is the moment we've been training for."

The creature stepped forward and entered the light of the fire. They could see its giant fangs and stare into its deadly eyes. The look on its face was one of death. Liam wasn't sure they could survive this fight and wondered if when Jrasta saw the creature in the light, he'd tell them all to retreat.

Jrasta looked up into the eyes of the beast. It bent down and bared its teeth and let out a vicious growl.

"Why, it's Mary!" Jrasta declared, sheathing his sword. "Why wake us up simply because Mary is here? You could have just told her we didn't need a ride!"

"What?" Liam replied. "That beast is named Mary? What kind of name is 'Mary' for a thing like that? Do you see the net full of people it's carrying?"

"Of course!" DOHNK replied. "She always carries people. She doesn't even charge for it. "I'm sorry, Mary. We don't need a ride anywhere tonight, but thank you so much for stopping by."

The beast nodded, but a tear began to roll down its cheek. "It's okay, little lady." As it spoke, the beast growled slowly in a voice which nearly shook the earth. It spoke with a slow, deep voice as if it had all the time in the world. "I don't want to bother you, but I wanted to check to see if you needed a ride." That's when the tears started pouring down so hard, Liam was afraid he might be in danger of being washed away. "But why did that little man have to attack me? He could have just told me you didn't want a ride. He didn't have to hit me with his sword. I mean, I would have just…"

With that, Mary lost it. She began weeping so hard and so loud that all the people in the net woke up and began talking to one another. "What's going on out there? Did someone hurt Mary?" "Why would someone hurt Mary? She's the sweetest person I know." "I don't know, but Mary's crying." "It's okay, Mary. Whatever it is, it'll be all right."

One of the people in the net called out, "Do you need a hug?"

"Yeeeeesssss," Mary replied.

With that, all the people crawled out of the net where they had been sleeping and came up to Mary. They all found a spot and snuggled in. Jrasta, Ezra, DOHNK and Jep moved up as well to give her a hug. Liam stood there for a moment and wondered what he should do. He felt really bad for hitting her with his sword, although he wondered if his sword had been hurt worse than she had been. He also thought it was perfectly reasonable that he thought she was an enemy. Finally, he spoke up. "I'm sorry, Mary. I didn't know who you were and I thought you were going to hurt my friends. That's why I attacked you."

"I forgive you, little man. Come and give me a hug. It'll make us both feel better," Mary said, slowly.

Everyone looked back at Liam expectantly. He shook his head and walked over to her. He nestled in for a big long hug. He was surprised at how warm and cuddly she was for a scaly beast of a creature.

The hug lasted an uncomfortably long time, and Liam was beginning to think they would have to spend the day hugging her to make her feel better, but after about thirty minutes or so, Mary said, "Thanks, everyone. You make me feel so loved."

The people all assured her of their undying love as they returned to the net, piling up on top of one another. Mary said goodbye to the team and then started dragging the net of people down the road, back toward where the guard's camp was.

Jrasta turned to Liam with an angry look on his face. "Liam. I hope you're proud of yourself. It's not every day that someone makes Mary cry. All she's doing is trying to help people out with free transportation along the king's highways, and you go ahead and try to cut off her hand!" He shook his head and turned to the rest of the group, "Well everyone, since we're up and the sun will be up shortly, why don't we grab a bite to eat and get on our way."

With that, the group found some breakfast, packed up and climbed up on their horses. Everyone still seemed a little upset at Liam for being so mean to Mary.

15. The Guards

As they rode along the path, Liam saw the sun begin to peek above the horizon. The air was quite chilly, but there was very little breeze. They moved quite fast, although not as fast as they had been the previous evening. The horses trotted along at a good speed and Liam suspected Lenny could keep that pace for quite a while.

They traveled in silence, still a little sleepy from being awakened so early. His friends appeared to be still grumpy about the idea that someone could try to hurt sweet, kind, gentle Mary. Liam was somewhat torn. On the one hand, he felt guilty because he had attacked Mary. On the other hand, there was nothing at all about that experience that might have suggested to him that Mary wasn't a threat to him and his team. He knew one thing, at least. He wanted to get this quest done so he could get back to the real world.

He was awakened from his daydream by the sound of galloping horses and the yells of a group of men. Before he realized what was happening, he and his friends were surrounded by the twelve guards. The guards had obviously gotten up early as well and had galloped here to catch up. Their horses panted heavily and looked about ready to collapse. All the soldiers had their swords out. They were ready for a fight.

Liam hadn't realized he had drawn his sword, but it was in his hand. Out of the corner of his eye, he could see the rest of his friends had also drawn their weapons. His heart beat rapidly. One look at Ezra and he saw a look of excitement mixed with sheer terror! Ezra was always on the lookout for a chance for adventure, and this was certainly it.

"Hello, Sergeant. Nice day for a ride, wouldn't you say?" Jrasta said through clenched teeth. He looked like he was ready to spring into action at any moment.

"It is a nice day for a ride, Jrasta. It's quite a surprise, meeting you out here," Sergeant Dimmock replied, appearing just as tense.

"Alright, those were our pleasantries. What do you want?" Jrasta wasn't one for small talk. Liam wasn't sure he was one for much conversation at all.

"I want the key. And I want the five of you to turn around and head back to Kings-Home so we can finish the quest without you getting in the way." The rest of the guards laughed.

"Tell you what," Jrasta said as he put his sword away and began to pick at his nails. It gave the illusion he wasn't too worried about the twelve guards. "Let's hop down off our horses and go have a chat."

The Sergeant looked skeptical, but after a moment's pause nodded his head. His soldiers immediately dismounted and led their horses over to a fallen log and tied them up.

Jrasta hopped down, and the rest followed his example. He handed the reins to Liam and told him to tie up the horses and then join him for a chat with the soldiers. Liam and the others led their horses toward the log at first, but Jep gave them the stink-eye. He gestured over to a few trees by the side of the road, and Liam realized if they had to make a break for it, this would be a better spot. It was a little farther down the path and in the direction they wanted to go. Jep looked at Liam, and he realized he shouldn't tie up the horses tightly, but in such a way that they could simply mount and run.

As they moved over to Jrasta and the guards, he noticed that Jrasta had picked a spot where he could sit with his back to a rather large rock. Liam, Ezra and DOHNK took their seats by him. Out of the corner of his eye, Liam noticed Jep down by the soldier's horses. He wondered what Jep might be doing down there, but in a few minutes, Jep had joined them as well.

"So here's what I'm thinking…" Jrasta continued to clean his nails and occasionally bite the odd one. "I'm thinking we should just continue on and not worry about each other. Up ahead the path divides. One way goes through the jungle, the other way down by the Achtor River. Why don't you head through the Jungle and we'll head down by the river? Both paths lead to the Sandy Desert and are roughly the same distance. This way, whoever gets there first will get the key… if they survive."

The Sergeant stared at Jrasta for a moment or two. He looked deep in thought about what Jrasta had suggested. "I don't like that idea. If you get there first, you'll get the key."

Jrasta stared back for a moment before replying. "Yes, I suppose you're right at that. Do you have another plan?"

"I sure do! We deal with you here and now!" Sergeant Dimmock stood up, followed by all his soldiers. They drew their swords and clearly planned on using them this time.

Liam realized with the stone to their back they had nowhere to run, but at the same time, they couldn't be surrounded again as they had been on horseback. His sword was out, and so were everyone else's.

"Remember your training, boys, and this will go just fine," DOHNK whispered to them. "Jrasta may not have told you this, but the two of you are fast learners and quite good with the sword. I don't think you'll have too much trouble with the guards. They are known for strength, not brains or skill. Use your head and your skill, and you'll be fine."

Liam was afraid that since there were twelve guards and only five of them, if you included Jep in that number, that he might be facing two or three guards, but only one approached him. He quickly glanced around to see where the others were. Ezra had a rather tall and solid looking guard approaching him, and DOHNK had a smaller, weak looking man approaching her. Liam suspected that the man thought she would be easy to overpower. Liam started to smile at that thought and even felt a little sorry for the man. Jrasta himself faced the Sergeant.

The other eight guards seemed to be clustered together and gathered around... Liam looked with horror at the eight of them converging on poor little Jep! He just about ran over to help his friend when the soldier before him attacked.

The man was huge, and Liam's first thought was that he was about to die. He quickly remembered what DOHNK had told him, "Remember your training."

The first attack came quickly and hard. Liam had learned you couldn't just stop the swing of a sword, especially if the one who wielded the sword was a giant brute of a man who looked like he could pick up a car. What kind of horse could carry this man? Liam started to daydream about the man riding a rhinoceros, as he used his own sword to slide the guard's sword off to one side. He waited for the next blow. It came a moment later, and Liam easily deflected this one in the same way. He realized DOHNK was right. The soldier was strong, but he had no skill whatsoever. He looked out of the corner of his eye and was relieved to see that none of the rest of his friends were having trouble with their opponents. Liam decided to put some of his skill to the test and easily disarmed the man. The guard's sword landed on the ground by his feet, and Liam quickly grabbed it and threw it into a grove of trees a short distance away.

Liam thought the man might surrender or maybe even beg for mercy. He thought the man might even stand there stunned that a young guy like Liam could disarm him so easily. Instead, the man started crying like a little baby and ran after his weapon. This, Liam did not expect. The whole battle had taken only a matter of seconds, and now the man had just run off into the woods in tears!

Liam remembered Jep. He looked around, terrified of what he might find. He searched the area with his eyes as he tried to see where the little chicken was. He hoped beyond hope that Jep was still alive. What he saw horrified him.

It wasn't that he was horrified because he saw his friend hurt or in danger. He was horrified at the sight of Jep, with his two little spears, in attack mode! He had no idea his little friend could move so fast and be so dangerous! Liam understood why eight guards had all converged on him. They knew the only chance they'd have against him was if he was hopelessly outnumbered.

Jep moved like lightning. He was a blur all around the guards. He jabbed them in the arm, then the leg, then the butt, then the ear. He seemed to enjoy going for the ears. By the time Liam began to watch the fight, each of the eight guards had at least two new piercings in each ear. Four of the guards were down and clearly weren't moving. Liam didn't think they were dead, just unconscious. The other four were trying to get away from him, but he moved so fast that every direction they ran, they ran into him. They began to cry out for help, but no guard was foolish enough to come to their aid.

Liam saw one of the guards he thought was unconscious raise his head and look around for a moment before he put his head down again. Liam was shocked to realize that most or all of the men he thought were unconscious were just pretending to be knocked out to save themselves from Jep's attack. One of the guards still on his feet suddenly dropped to the ground and wouldn't move. He joined the rest of his friends as he faked unconsciousness.

Once Jep was done, he turned his attention to the other soldiers. None of them were a problem for Ezra, Jrasta or DOHNK, but once Jep arrived on the scene, all three were down in a matter of seconds. It was at this time that Liam's opponent emerged from the grove of trees, holding his sword by the blade. He swung it all around while he yelled some kind of war-cry which sounded somewhat like a burp. Liam realized it wasn't a war-cry at all, but in fact was a burp. It was significantly less threatening than it may have been intended. He charged Liam, but out of the corner of his eye, he noticed the other eleven soldiers lying unconscious (or pretending to be so). He came to a stop and slowly got down on to his knees, then fully on the ground. He didn't move again as long as Liam and the others were there.

Jrasta looked around to make sure every one of his friends was okay. Once he saw no one was hurt, he pointed at the horses, and they made their way there. They each quickly climbed up into the saddle.

Jrasta told them to wait a moment and turned and rode back toward the guards. They still lay motionless on the ground. He went directly to the soldier's mounts and yelled really loud, slapping some of them and chasing them off. This got the guards' attention, and some of them got to their feet. They chased after the horses but were too slow. Their mounts rode off in every single direction. Jrasta galloped over to Liam and the others and yelled, "Let's move!"

"So that's what Jep was doing over by their horses. He was untying them all?" Liam asked, impressed at how that all happened.

"When you've ridden together as often as Jep and I have, you learn a thing or two about dealing with soldiers and others who want to take advantage of you." Jrasta laughed, and Jep joined in. Liam felt somewhat disturbed by the sight of a chicken laughing.

After they had galloped for a few minutes, the group slowed down to an easy trot. "No use wearing out our horses, folks. Let's take it easy for a bit. The guards will be a while gathering up their mounts, and by then we'll be at the crossroads."

Liam remembered there were two routes: the jungle route and the river route. Jrasta had suggested they take the river route and the soldiers take the jungle route.

"So we're taking the river road?" Liam asked.

"No, we will take the road through the jungle. The guards will take the river road." Jrasta explained.

Liam looked confused. "I thought you told them they should take the jungle and we should take the river road. What if they take the jungle road and follow after us?"

"They won't, Liam. No worries there. I recommended that they take the jungle and we take the river. The Sergeant isn't the brightest man I've ever met, and it's easy to figure out what he'll do. Since I suggested he take the jungle road, he'll think I suggested they head that way because it's dangerous and hard and we were going to take the river road because it's easy and safe."

"Is it? Is the river road safe?" Liam asked.

"Nope, it's pretty dangerous, and it's hard going. The road sometimes gets washed out, and there are a lot of dangers along the way. The jungle road is dangerous too, but nothing like the river road. They won't know what hit them! If, however, the Sergeant wants to harm us and plans on following us where we are going, he thinks we're going down the river road since I suggested it and he'll go that way so he can catch us and attack. Still, we'll be on different roads, and he'll have a tough journey ahead of him." Jrasta seemed quite pleased with himself.

"What if he suspects we're trying to trick him and takes the jungle road?" Liam thought he'd push Jrasta's plan a little bit.

"Never gonna happen!" Jrasta laughed. "The Sergeant may be in charge of those troops, and he may fancy himself a decent advisor to the throne, but he's not the sharpest guy. He won't think that deeply. If he does, he'll just confuse himself, get mad and try to chase us down the river road. We won't see them for a while."

Liam figured this was one of those things with which he should just trust Jrasta. It was good to have the soldiers behind them. Liam felt better being able to put them out of his mind for a little while.

16. The Dark Jungle

They continued down the road. It was good to be back on the path again after their detour to the Lizard Men Village. The path was smooth, well-worn and, since Mary had just been through this way dragging her giant net of people, quite clear of any obstructions. Liam wondered how it felt to be on the bottom of that net, with a bunch of people smooshed on top of you and then to be dragged along the ground.

As they moved farther along the path, they came to a rise in the road. Coming to the top, Liam found he was able to see out over the land for miles in all directions. Ahead of them and a little to the South of them, the Achtor River ran from the East, flowing back toward the West. As he twisted around to look back along the West, he could see it turned slightly South after a little ways. It was a huge river, wide enough in spots that it might even be mistaken for a lake. On the other side of the river, Liam could see a mountain range spread out into the distance, many of the snow-capped peaks hidden in the clouds.

On this side of the river, just a short distance ahead of them, Liam could see the path split off to the right and become what Jrasta had called the River Road. From this distance, the River Road didn't appear too dangerous, but he remembered Jrasta's description of that way. The path also split off to the left and disappeared into a large forest with massive trees. Liam assumed this was the jungle Jrasta had spoken about.

In less than an hour, they came upon the point where the path split. There were no signs to indicate where each path might lead. Without a word, Jrasta led them to the left, and the path became steeper as it climbed toward the forest. Liam had to work hard to keep from sliding off Lenny, but the horses did not appear to struggle.

Liam looked up ahead at the forest, admiring the huge trees. He had never seen trees that large before.

Jrasta spoke up, interrupting his thoughts. "We're just about at the Dark Jungle. Be careful, everyone. There are some dangerous man-eating beasts in there. We need to stick close together. There is safety in numbers. Don't stray away from the group at any cost!" Jrasta warned them. "Should be fun!"

They rode on for a while in silence. Liam took in the sights and watched the trees get closer. After some time, Liam grew tired of the quiet. He wanted to make some conversation. He knew whenever he did this with this group, it left him frustrated, and something told him he should just keep quiet. He decided to ignore that little voice inside his head which told him he'd be frustrated with this conversation and spoke up anyway.

"So, why do they call it the Dark Jungle?" Liam didn't really care to know, nor did he think it was all that important, but he hoped a conversation would be fun.

"What would make you think there is any reason why it would be called the Dark Jungle?" Jrasta asked, as he pulled out a pipe and popped it in his mouth. Liam had never seen him smoke a pipe before and Jrasta didn't seem like a pipe kind of guy. After he popped it in, he pulled a small flask out of his shirt, unscrewed the top and poured a little in the end. In a few seconds, Liam realized the liquid was soap of some kind as Jrasta began blowing bubbles into the air. Jrasta had a pipe for blowing bubbles. Odd, but not surprising.

Liam watched the bubbles for a few seconds before he responded. "I don't know. I would just think that if someone came up with a name for something like the 'Dark' Jungle, there would be some reason for calling it 'Dark.'"

Jrasta considered that for a moment before responding. "Sometimes, Liam, you make no sense whatsoever. Why does there have to be a reason for the name?"

"I don't know! Why didn't they call it the Fun Jungle or the Happy Jungle? Why not call it the Tasty Jungle or the Stinky Jungle? Or why not just plain, Jungle?" Liam felt that familiar frustration begin to grow inside of him.

"Well, those are pretty dumb names," Jrasta said as he blew more bubbles into the air from his pipe. The others looked over at Liam like he wasn't making sense.

"Why is it dumb?" Liam asked.

"Well, what's happy about it? If you call it the Happy Jungle, shouldn't it be happy?" Jrasta rolled his eyes.

"I don't know what's happy about it! Tell me what's dark about it! If you call it the Dark Jungle, shouldn't it be dark?" Liam felt his argument was pretty solid, or it would be anywhere else. Sadly, he knew he was still in for a world of frustration. He just couldn't seem to stop himself.

"I don't think you're making any sense, Liam. I think we should just drop this and head into the Dark Jungle." Ezra said as he brought his horse up beside Liam. "If you keep going with these strange arguments, you're just going to embarrass yourself more."

"Fine. Forget I brought it up." Liam wondered why he bothered with these conversations. Sometimes he thought it would be best if he didn't ask any more questions.

By this point, they had come to the edge of the jungle, and Jrasta spoke up. "Alright everyone, remember, keep close. This is a dangerous jungle, and as we get in there, you'll find the trees block out the sun. It'll be hard to see one another during the day and nearly impossible at night. It's pretty dark in there."

Liam just hung his head in frustration and muttered to himself, "why... why... why...?"

The jungle itself started rather abruptly. The path just prior to this point had been in open land with few bushes or trees at all, but when the jungle began, it was like a solid wall of trees and bushes. The only way into this mess of growth was the path. It was only wide enough for two to ride side by side, so they crammed in close together and entered in.

It certainly was dark, and to Liam, it was obvious the jungle had come by its name honestly. The trunks of the trees were larger than any he had ever seen, and they stood taller than any trees back home. They seemed to stretch up forever, and the tops were lost in a dark haze, creating a canopy for the forest. He could hear noises come from the jungle. Sometimes there was the sound of an animal which called out to another and Liam could hear a response follow right after, somewhere off in the darkness. Sometimes he heard growls. Sometimes he would hear the sound of a very large creature as it crashed through the trees and plants. This place was more alive than any place they'd been so far.

Since they could not see the sun, they had to use their stomachs as their clock. Once all of them could hear growls from their bellies, they realized it was lunchtime. They stopped for a quick bite, but only long enough to get their food out of their packs and into their mouths.

They continued along the way. The path wound through the trees. At times, they could see the glow of eyes in the woods, watching them from a distance. Liam wondered what kind of creature it could be and if it was friendly or dangerous.

By supper time, when their bellies started to growl again, they were ready for a break. They found an area where the path was a little wider, and they thought they could set up camp. They hopped down, built a small fire and got ready for supper. The fire was small but seemed to burn like the sun. After being in such a dark forest all day, it was hard to look at the flames at first. In time their eyes adjusted and they were able to relax a little bit. The light from the fire gave such a sense of safety.

They cooked a meal for themselves and then, as was their pattern each day, they took out their swords and began to practice. It was much harder to practice by firelight since the flames would flicker and shadows would grow and move around them. At first, Liam and Ezra thought they should skip their practice while in the jungle, but Jrasta explained it was good for them to learn to fight when light was scarce.

By the time they finished, Liam, Ezra, Jrasta and DOHNK were all sweaty, and Liam could smell how badly he stunk. The Jungle itself was quite warm. There was very little air movement, but loads of humidity. Everything felt wet, and Liam seemed to sweat more than usual. This only added to the smell, but he wondered if, in a fight, he could use his body odor to his advantage. It was, after all, pretty gross.

As he was about to lie down for the night, Liam once again noticed the eyes upon them. They were closer this time, and he could tell they belonged to a rather large beast.

He pointed the eyes out to Jrasta who jumped to his feet in alarm. "Everyone, arm yourselves!"

135

The eyes moved quickly toward them. There was the sound of a large beast as it crashed through the forest. It came closer and closer. Whatever this creature was, it sounded nasty!

As it came out onto the path, only a few steps from them, Liam and the others were filled with dread. The creature moved on all fours with yellow fur covering its entire body. It was about the size of a large ape and had claws and teeth which gave the impression it was not to be messed with. It paced back and forth on the path, clearly ready to attack. Liam didn't remember having drawn his sword or his knife, but both weapons were in his hands.

"This is one of those man-eating beasts I told you about," Jrasta began, speaking quietly as if he was concerned about upsetting the creature. "We're going to have to move carefully if we're going to survive this experience. If we don't give it what it wants, it will attack."

Liam thought that was an odd statement to make. If this was a man-eating beast, why would they give it what it wanted? How could they give it what it wanted? He hoped Jrasta didn't intend to feed one of them to this beast so it wouldn't attack.

"This is what we're going to do. I want each of you to grab some man and toss it over to the beast. When it gets what it wants, it should leave us alone," Jrasta said. He didn't take his eyes off the beast the entire time he spoke.

Liam thought this was also an odd statement to make. He had gotten somewhat used to some of the odd things said here in this world, but he was also a little worried that he might, in fact, be the "man" everyone would decide to grab and toss to the beast. He wondered if his friends would really hand him over to the beast. What kind of a crazy world was this?

He turned his head slightly to see what everyone else was doing and was surprised to see them running around the fire. As they ran, they ripped up plants out of the ground. The beast looked on as they moved. It continued to growl and snort and pace back and forth.

"What are you doing?" Liam asked. He felt angry at them for weeding the path at a time like this.

"Man only grows on the forest floor, Liam! Get pulling it up! If we don't give the beast enough, it'll attack!" DOHNK hollered back at Liam.

"These plants are called 'man'?" Liam asked, a little angry, but also quite relieved. "You mean when Jrasta called this beast a man-eating beast, he meant it ate this plant? A plant called 'man'?"

"Of course, what did you think I meant?" Jrasta replied. "Get to work! If the man-eaters don't get their plants, they turn into person-eaters, and that's not good for us!"

Liam knelt down and began to pull up and collect plants. He loaded up his arms with the green weeds. As he collected the "man," he wondered what a "person" was. Were they the "persons" or was that some other kind of plant. This world seemed to be designed around the idea of confusion. He muttered to himself while he worked, "You don't think this is a little on the confusing side?"

"What's that, Liam?" Ezra asked.

"Nothing! Just pulling up man!" Liam didn't want another conversation about dumb stuff.

When they had each gathered an armful, they walked up to the beast and dropped what they had collected before the creature. It watched them warily at first, but when the last of them had dropped their load, the beast attacked the man and scarfed it all down.

When it was finished, it lunged at Jrasta and began to lick his face. It then turned to DOHNK, Ezra, Jep and then Liam last of all. Liam, like everyone else, was left dripping with man-flavored slobber. The beast turned back toward the darkness of the jungle and crashed off into the trees.

"I'm glad that's dealt with," Jrasta announced. "Now that the man-eater has been fed, we should be able to get a good night's sleep. He'll think of us as friends for now and patrol around the campsite for us. We should be safe till morning."

The word, "should," didn't make Liam feel all that safe, but he knew better than to question this before bed. It would only lead to more frustration. His own.

17. The Fortress

The next day was dark. Liam lay there, listening to the man-eater crash through the jungle all around their camp, presumably scaring away dangerous creatures. It was difficult to tell what time of the day it was, other than to say that the sun was up. There was at least a little bit of light coming through the trees.

His nose hurt. It wasn't the kind of hurt one might feel if one had a cold. It was, instead, the kind of hurt one might feel if a chicken had latched onto one's nose.

Liam groaned. It had been days since Jep latched on like this and Liam had hoped Jep had given up on his desire to eat his snozzle. Jep appeared to be still asleep from the sound of the snoring coming from the chicken and Liam wondered if he could simply pry him off. He reached around the floor of the jungle and found a little twig which he stuck in Jep's beak and began to pry open his mouth. Within minutes he was free, but his nose didn't feel quite right.

The rest of the group started moving, and within a few minutes, Jrasta had stoked the fire. It was good to have some light and be able to see what they were doing. They made themselves a small breakfast and began packing up camp.

Once they were loaded up and had put out the fire, they began moving down the path once again. Jrasta explained to them what lay ahead. "I haven't been through the entire Jungle before. I've just been a little farther on from here, and I turned around. There is a cliff face that runs through the center of the jungle, and there is only one way up to the other side. It's through an old fortress built into the rock."

"What made you turn around?" Ezra asked. Liam was thrilled that he wasn't the only one asking questions today. Whenever he asked a simple question, he would get a silly answer or be told he was being unreasonable. He was happy to let someone else deal with Jrasta's frustratingly unclear answers for once.

"It's really dangerous," Jrasta answered clearly.

Liam decided maybe this was his chance for a clear answer himself. "What kind of danger?" he asked.

"The kind that you could get hurt with," Jrasta answered. "What kind of a question is that, Liam?"

Liam groaned to himself, but let it go.

Jrasta continued. "The old fortress was built here years ago as a way to defend the pass from invading armies. Since it's in the Dark Jungle and no one wanted to come here, they put all sorts of traps throughout the passage to the top of the cliff in order to keep enemies from making it through alive. It's an unmanned fortress. There are pressure plates that activate traps. There are floors that collapse when you try to walk on them. There are spikes that come out of the wall and can skewer you. I hear there are even giant feet that will come out of the ceiling and step on you."

"This is safer than the river road?" Liam asked, finding it hard to believe that they were coming this way.

"Absolutely. Few people survive the journey down the river road. Your chances of making it along that path alive are very slim." Jrasta said, looking around for signs of danger.

"What are the chances of making it through this fortress alive?" Liam asked.

"Don't know. So far no one has survived, so it's hard to say. Hopefully, we will be the first. Once someone makes it through alive, we can figure out what the chances are. Till then, it's anyone's guess what the odds might be."

Liam thought that one through a little bit. Part of him wanted to turn around and ride in the opposite direction, but he did have to complete this quest before the Regent's guards found the key and returned it.

Before long, they saw what appeared to be a large wall ahead of them. Through the darkness, it began to take shape, and they could see it was a cliff of solid stone. There would be no way they could climb it, let alone get the horses up it. As they looked directly ahead, however, there was in fact what appeared to be a large castle built into the side of the cliff with a single open door leading into it. The castle had two towers, one on each side of the door, and many windows. The castle was built all the way up to the top of the cliff.

The path led right up to the open entrance. It didn't look overly inviting as the doorway led into pitch darkness. Liam felt fear growing in his heart as he looked at the door. Who knew what might be on the other side of that dark opening? As he glanced around, it appeared that Ezra and DOHNK had the same feelings.

"Alright, hop down everyone. We have to go through on foot from here. The horses won't be able to climb through the passageways. They have to take a different route." Jrasta said.

They each climbed down off their mounts and led the horses forward. Before they entered the fortress, Jrasta bent down and grabbed a few small rocks from the ground. They were around the size of his fist. He pocketed the rocks but didn't explain why he had collected them.

They entered the doorway, and Liam found the room to have so little light, he could barely make out anything beyond just a step in front of him. Just inside the door was a rack with a series of sticks on them. Jrasta crouched down on the floor and with his flint, started a small fire. He pulled out one of the sticks from the rack and lit it to use as a torch. It gave off a great deal of light. He passed that torch on to DOHNK and lit another. This one he gave to Ezra and then one each for himself and Liam. He then put out the little fire he'd made.

From the light of the torches, they could see a little more of where they were. The room was a decent size, but the only furniture was the rack with the unlit torches. Straight ahead was a set of stairs going up and off to the left was a large sliding doorway. Behind them lay the entrance they had come through. Apart from this, there were no features or windows.

He led them off to the left to the room behind the sliding door. They followed Jrasta's example of leading the horses into the small room, just large enough for the four horses to fit and they all stepped out. Jrasta closed the door and pressed a button labeled, "UP." The sound of a motor kicked in, and through the openings in the door, Liam could see the four horses moving upwards.

"So, the horses have an elevator up to the top?" Liam asked, a little surprised at everything from the fact that there was an elevator here with a motor (which was the first technology he'd seen since his arrival in this world) to the fact that they didn't seem to be using it for themselves. He knew this would be thought of as a dumb question by the rest of the group, but he had to ask. "Does this elevator go right to the top and avoid all the traps and dangers of the fortress?"

"Of course! The horses don't deserve to be hurt by flying spears or collapsing floors. The door will open at the top, and the horses will exit. If we don't survive, they'll be free to find a new home." Jrasta turned and started toward the stairs on the other side of the room.

"If the elevator avoids all the dangers, why don't we take it to the top and maybe we can live through this?" Liam stood there. He didn't want to take the stairs if that route was so dangerous.

"Ahh… for once you have asked a good question, Liam! I apologize, I obviously wasn't clear. The elevator is a horse elevator. NOT a human elevator. Well, let's get going!"

Liam watched his friends disappear up the stairs. He didn't like this at all but figured he stood a better chance with the group than apart from them. Besides, he suspected the horse elevator was designed in a way which would not allow a human to use it. Somehow that made sense in this upside down world. He hurried up the stairs after his friends.

He caught up with the others as they stood at the entrance to a large square room with an open door on the far side. Jrasta stood there and explained the danger to the group. "So each room is like a test. We have to figure out what the danger is, figure out how to get through it alive and then the hard part, we have to actually get through it alive. This room here, you see, is pretty simple. There are all sorts of holes in the walls along each side of the room. That tells you that something will shoot out of the holes in the walls at us, likely poisonous darts. They may kill us instantly, or we may have to suffer in absolute agony for days or weeks before succumbing to the poison. Simple! There will be something in the room that sets it off, and if we trigger it, we die. So, before stepping into this room, let's look around and see what we can learn."

Liam and Ezra crouched down while looking around. The holes were up around chest height, and Liam wondered if they were to move through the room on their hands and knees, if the darts would fire over their heads. They examined the room ahead of them for a trip wire, but there appeared to be no wires traveling through the room. Nothing looked out of place in the room, till Ezra noticed one of the stone tiles in the floor right in the center of the room appeared to be chipped along its edges. He pointed this out to Jrasta.

"That's it, my boy! Way to go! That must be a pressure plate!" Jrasta walked forward, stepped around the pressure plate and through to the other side. "Come on through, everyone! It's safe as long as you don't step on that tile."

They each made their way through the room. When they had all come to the other side and stepped out of the room, Jrasta reached into a pocket and pulled out one of the rocks he'd picked up on the way in. He tossed it into the room, and it landed on the tile. The moment it touched the pressure plate, hundreds of darts started flying out of the holes in the wall. There seemed to be no end to them and there appeared to be no place anywhere in the room that wasn't covered by one of the darts.

"Wow! Good eye, Ezra," DOHNK said. "I don't think we would have survived that room if you hadn't seen that tile. I wonder what's next!"

They followed the passage deeper into the side of the cliff. Doorways opened up now and then, and Jrasta explained that there were many routes to the top, each as deadly as the next. The walls along here were carved out of solid rock, rather than built with hewn stone like the previous rooms.

After a little ways, the passage opened up into a wide room. The walls and ceiling were featureless, except for a few fixtures on the walls for torches. There was a set of stairs going up on the far side. The floor itself was a mess of different colored tiles. The tiles were red, blue, yellow, green and brown. No one dared step into this room until they figured out the trap.

They looked for tiles which could be pressure plates. Nothing seemed odd about any of the tiles, other than the bright colors. There were no holes in the walls for darts. The ceiling was one piece with the walls so it didn't look like it could crumble down on them. That left one possibility. The floor was the problem. They had to figure this one out before they set foot in the room.

DOHNK was the first to come up with a solution. "I don't think we should step on any tiles at all. It could be all of the green ones or all of the red ones that trigger the trap. We just don't know! I have an idea."

She set down her pack and reached inside. Liam was surprised to see her pull out a crossbow from inside. She set an arrow in the crossbow and tied a rope to the back of it. Aiming across the room and toward the stairs, she fired the crossbow and to Liam's surprise, it sunk right into one of the steps of the stairs on the far side. She then turned around and tied the other end off on a fixture set in the wall for holding torches.

"There! Now we can slide across on this rope and not worry about touching the floor." She grabbed the rope, swung up and shimmied her way across the room.

Jrasta laughed to himself at her creativity and climbed up. He held on with his knees and hands and made his way across. Jep went next, balancing on the rope tight-rope style. Liam followed Jep and Ezra brought up the rear.

As Ezra moved his way across, the rope started to slip off the fixture where it was tied. He jolted downwards, and his legs swung out underneath him, hitting the floor hard. Without any further warning, the floor dropped down, swinging open like a set of doors with the hinges at the walls on either side. Ezra looked down below him, only to see a vast dark hole. There appeared to be no bottom. He quickly squirmed his way up onto the rope again, clinging with all his might.

He began to shimmy his way across the open chasm, clearly much more worried now that he could see the deep pit below him. The knot on the fixture shifted again, starting to come loose. Before anyone realized what was happening, the rope came undone, and Ezra swung downwards, clinging desperately to the rope.

Everyone grabbed the end of the rope attached to the arrow just in case it came loose as well. Liam dropped down on his belly and looked over the edge, screaming out, "Ezra! Are you okay?"

At first, there was no sound at all, and everyone feared Ezra had fallen to his death. A single tear rolled down Jep's face as they considered this possibility.

"I'm okay," came a weak voice from below. "Just really scared. Really, really scared."

Everyone breathed a sigh of relief and quickly began to pull the rope. When they saw him struggling at the edge, Liam grabbed his shirt and helped him up and over the edge. They hugged each other and cried a little, till they realized they were really uncomfortable with the idea of hugging and crying and quickly stepped back from one another.

The group stopped and took a little break there on the stairs, preparing themselves to move on. They hadn't brought much food, most of it was with the horses, but they had just enough to take a bit of a snack and still have some left over in case the trip through the fortress took longer than expected.

They resumed their climb up the stairs, and after a few steps, the stairs turned sharply to the left, climbing up again. At the base of this new set of stairs, the wall had a large, rather detailed picture of a skull. Jrasta mumbled something about that being a bad sign, and as they started up this set of stairs, Ezra asked if it was possible that the stairs were actually the next trap. This question was answered as Jrasta's foot landed on a step that moved... just slightly.

A loud rumble echoed down the stairway, and before they realized what was going on, the stairs had turned down. Each step angled downwards, forming a long slide. At first, they all began to slide while still on their feet, trying to hold on to the walls to slow their descent, but within seconds Jrasta toppled over and then knocked each one over in turn.

Liam was at the bottom of the group and looked behind him. Where the skull had been on the wall at the turn, there was now an opening. On the other side of the opening were giant wooden spikes! If they didn't stop soon, Liam would be the first one turned into Swiss cheese, and each one after would follow his example. They all realized at about the same moment the danger they were in. Liam pulled his knife out and began searching the slide and walls for anything he could stick it in to stop the descent. Finally, his knife slid into a hole, and he ground to a halt. Each person slammed into him and halted as well. It was a wonder Liam could hold on and a wonder the knife didn't break. They had all lost their torches. In the darkness, Liam stretched out his toes and felt the first of the spikes just below him.

Liam told them what he had done, and each one grabbed their knife and began to feel the walls and floor for grooves or holes they could use to climb up. Within seconds, Ezra had found holes set in the wall a little way up the side of the stairway. They were spaced perfectly for hands to grab. The five of them began to slowly make their way up the slide in the dark to the top using the hand holds.

When they reached the top, they could just barely make out a doorway a short distance away. They had made it to the exit of the Jungle Fortress. They were the first to make it through alive, and Liam and Ezra thought that was kind of a good thing.

As they found their way outside, the horses were easy to locate. The elevator had simply stopped at the top of the Fortress, and their mounts were safe and sound. The elevator had even provided them with some oats to munch on and some water, so the horses were well fed and ready to go.

18. The Sandy Desert

The way through the rest of the Jungle was pretty straightforward. There were no more man-eaters or fortresses. The path was pretty simple to follow and quite smooth. Now that they were up on top of the cliff, there was even a bit of a breeze which managed to make its way down the path. The breeze took the edge off of how hot and humid the jungle was. Within a short distance from the fortress, they could start to make out some more light ahead, and it wasn't long before they were at the edge of the jungle.

The jungle thinned out slowly on this side, as opposed to the other side where they had entered. The other side had gone from "not-jungle" to "total-jungle" in no time at all. The trees on this side grew farther apart, and Liam noticed they weren't quite as tall. The bushes and plant life on the floor of the jungle grew much more sparse here as well. As they traveled, the sounds of the jungle were heard less and less till there was only the sound of the occasional bird.

As they came out of the edge of the jungle, past the last of the trees, the path faded into a desert. Liam squinted as he looked around. As far as he could see there was nothing but sand, sand dunes, the occasional cactus, blue sky above and lots of heat. It was very hot.

Jrasta called them to a halt, and they led their horses back a little ways into the jungle, just enough to find some shade from the sun. They set up camp, even though it was only late afternoon, and put together a good hearty meal.

While they ate, Jrasta explained the path ahead. "We're about to enter the Sandy Desert. It's not the easiest part of Arestana to travel through, although it's only about a day's journey from one side to the other. The big problem with it is that it's really easy to get lost. When we're in the desert, there's no water, there's no sign of a path, and there are lots of scorpions. Many people have died in this desert, and the sand just covers them up. If we die out there, there will be no one to find us. They call it the Sandy Desert after the first person who died trying to cross it. Her name was Sandy."

"We're going to rest well tonight and rise early tomorrow morning. We will head out early before the sun is at its hottest point. We'll head straight east across the desert, keeping the mountains to the north of us and the sun before us as it rises. There won't be a chance for a break, and if you hop down from your horse, the scorpions will get you. Any questions?"

Liam and Ezra looked at each other. This didn't sound like it was going to be their favorite section of the journey.

No one had any questions. They ate in silence, thinking ahead to their journey the next day.

That night they practiced with their swords again. They even worked on a little hand-to-hand combat. Liam and Ezra had improved a lot, and both Jrasta and DOHNK were excellent teachers.

The next morning, Jep woke them up while it was still dark. Liam and Ezra tended to put their bedrolls side by side at night. When Jep came near to wake them, he crouched down between them and crowed as loud as he could. Both boys woke up when they heard the noise and thought they were under attack. They screamed, jumped out of their blankets, grabbed their swords and started to swing them while they yelled to anyone and everyone, "We surrender! We surrender!!!"

Jep looked at them with laughing eyes and then wandered over to DOHNK. Somehow she had slept through the noise. Jep woke her up with a gentle caress across her cheek with his wing. She looked up at him peacefully and thanked him.

Jrasta was already up and had breakfast made. They gobbled down their meal, packed up the supplies, loaded their horses and mounted. In no time at all, they were on their way.

The first few hours were quite nice. The sun hadn't risen yet and, although it was a little chilly, it felt good to be on their horses. As the sun came up, it was directly in their eyes and seemed especially bright over the sand. Within a short while, the temperature started to rise, and Liam started to sweat. He began to realize how badly he needed another bath. The stink was bad. He wasn't the only one, either. Now and then a waft of stink would hit him from Ezra's direction. Ezra didn't seem to enjoy the smell much more than Liam. Liam could see his friend trying to figure out if the smell was him or his horse. Sadly, the horses smelled quite lovely compared to the boys.

They passed dune after dune with no real sign of an end. The only clues they had for direction were the mountains to their left and the position of the sun.

Finally, Jrasta called out that it was time for lunch. Liam and Ezra immediately started to climb down from their horses, but Jrasta hollered at them to stop. "What are you doing? Don't you remember what I told you about the scorpions?"

Liam looked down at the ground, and it looked like the sand was moving, just a little bit. As he stared at it, he began to realize that the sand was covered with tiny little light brown or yellow scorpions, no bigger than a plum. They didn't seem to bother with the horses, but Jrasta told them that they despised people and they would not hesitate to sting someone repeatedly.

"I don't think you'd like getting stung by one of these," Jrasta warned them. "But you'd probably be okay. The problem is that they swarm people. Must be something in the smell of people that drives them crazy. If you put one foot down in that sand, they will come after you so fast and cover you so completely, we'd probably never see you again, just a pile of scorpions."

They reached around in their saddles and grabbed their provisions. They ate lunch as they rode and continued their journey.

The afternoon went much like the morning had, just hotter and the sun was behind them. Liam realized he had not yet ridden Lenny this long without a break. He found his legs beginning to cramp up a bit and his butt cried out for a break. Lenny seemed to manage just fine.

As the sun started to get low in the late afternoon, Liam noticed something up ahead as he crested the top of a particularly high sand dune. It stuck up out of the sand, was a darker color and ran right across the horizon.

Ezra saw it as well. "Jrasta, I see something up ahead! Is that the end of the desert?"

"It's close. We're nearly there. There is a ridge of rocky ground running through the edge of the Sandy Desert. If we can survive that, then there is just a little bit of desert on the other side before we get back on solid ground. When we get there, we can search for the pit where Kenny the Dragon lives."

"This ridge is dangerous? What's so dangerous about it?" Ezra asked, getting that look in his eye he would often get. It was one of fear mixed with excitement. Ezra tended to be happiest when things were dangerous.

"Well, I told you this was the Sandy Desert, right? Lots of people have died in this desert, but there's something about this place where the bones of the person who died end up here at this ridge. Once the bones arrive here, they come alive again and attack anyone who tries to cross over to the other side. Kind of like the desert's last attempt to finish you off before you get on with your journey." Jrasta chuckled to himself like this was all just good fun.

Liam had long since learned that to ask a question, challenge anything or clarify any details was a foolish venture, but still found he couldn't let most things go. "So, we just have to battle a whole bunch of zombie skeletons intent on killing us off, climb down into a deep pit, slay a dragon without getting eaten and then we're home free?"

"Whoa, whoa, whoa! Liam, don't jump to conclusions! Where did this dragon come from?" Everyone looked at Liam again like he was dumb. He thought perhaps he was getting used to it.

"The Regent described a large beast, covered in scales. It breathes fire and is named Kenny the Dragon. That doesn't seem to you like he might be a dragon… named Kenny?" Liam wondered why he even bothered, but he was upset they had to battle skeletons, and he wanted to take it out on someone.

"Kenny the Dragon… well, I guess I can see why someone might jump to that conclusion… if they didn't stop to think it all through. Liam, you should stop making assumptions like that. Just because this guy is named Kenny the Dragon doesn't mean he's actually a dragon. Did you know that Jep's full name is 'Jep the Chicken'? But he's clearly a Rooster! Try to make fewer assumptions, and you won't look so foolish!"

"But a rooster is a… oh never mind." Liam bit his tongue and decided to let it go.

By this point, they had arrived at the ridge of rocky ground. After the conversations Liam had with Jrasta about Kenny the Dragon and the Dark Jungle, it was a surprise that the ridge of rocky ground was in fact rocky… and a ridge.

Liam looked down at where the ground met the sand. The layer of little yellow scorpions stopped at the edge of the sand. Jrasta hopped down just inches from the scorpions, but not one made any move toward him. He drew his sword and started up the ridge. He led his horse behind him. The rest of the group followed his lead.

At first, there was no sign of skeletons. Liam hoped they could make it right across without meeting any at all. It didn't look like the ridge was all that large, perhaps maybe a five minute walk from one side to the other. He thought maybe if they were really quiet, the skeletons might not notice them.

Jrasta began to sing in a really loud and off-key voice. Liam had not realized it was possible to be that off-key. His voice was like a cat, stuck inside a vacuum.

Liam shushed him right away. "Jrasta, aren't you afraid the skeletons will hear you? They'll hear you sing and come attack us! If we're quiet, maybe we can make it through here without being noticed."

Jrasta stopped his song and gave Liam a look. Liam had learned to recognize that look from many difficult conversations over the last number of days. "Liam, how many skeletons do you know who have ears?"

Liam let that one sink in for a moment before he replied. "Good point."

Jrasta started to sing again, if it could be called singing. Ezra and DOHNK joined in, somehow managing to recognize the tune. DOHNK had a voice like an angel… if that angel was in agony from getting her toe caught in a mouse trap. Ezra was the only one with a decent voice. He sounded like he could actually carry a tune. Unfortunately, he seemed to have absolutely no sense of rhythm. He would sing faster than the others, then slower, then faster. Right words, right tune, just faster and then slower than anyone else. Jep was the last one to join in. He sang just like one might expect a rooster to sing. Or maybe more like an angry rooster as it hollered at a dog which had come too close to the hen house. It wasn't good.

Finally, Liam decided to sing as well. He just picked a song he liked and started in, loud and proud. The rest of the group stopped the moment he began to sing, resulting in the first and only line of his song being a solo.

"I think I see movement up ahead. They might have heard us coming," Jrasta whispered. This annoyed Liam to no end.

Sure enough, Liam could see movement a short distance away. It looked like rocks and dirt were shifting back and forth. A hand appeared, then an arm, then a shoulder. None of what Liam saw was covered in skin, just bone. Other hands started emerging from the ground, and entire skeletons began to climb to their feet. Liam was shocked to think this many people could have died in the Sandy Desert. He didn't want to be one of them.

Liam, Ezra and the others drew their swords and prepared for battle. Liam worried about Lenny and the rest of the horses. He wasn't sure what would happen to them in the fight. He wasn't the only one with this on his mind.

"How do we protect the horses through this fight?" DOHNK asked.

Without taking his eyes off the skeletons, Jrasta replied, "They'll ignore the horses. They're like the scorpions. The horses aren't of interest. The skeletons just want us. Nothing else."

"I think I feel so much better," DOHNK said to no one in particular. "How do we kill these skeletons?"

Jrasta looked at her with the look he usually reserved for Liam. "DOHNK! Did you seriously just ask me how to kill a bunch of skeletons?" Liam didn't want bad things for DOHNK, but it did feel good knowing he wasn't the only one asking the most obvious

155

questions and getting a frustrating answer. "DOHNK," Jrasta continued, "sometimes you amaze me. After all the dumb questions I've received from Liam and Ezra, you come out and ask the most brilliant question imaginable. Well done!"

Liam rolled his eyes.

"Here's what we do. Spread out and watch each other's back. The skeletons only have one real weakness. They don't like anyone pointing out that they look too skinny. They are very sensitive about their weight and too many comments, either positive or negative, cause them to simply collapse. But if you don't get them down fast enough, they will swarm you and drag you back to the sand where they toss you to the scorpions. Use your swords to knock them back to give you more time to talk." Jrasta took up position at the front of the group and prepared for the onslaught.

Liam began to think through what he would say, not entirely sure he was comfortable with this. He had naturally avoided any comments about people's weight as he thought it was rude, so he didn't have a list prepared. He readied himself.

Jrasta struck first with a real humdinger of a comment. "Hey, you guys look like you missed breakfast. You know it's the most important meal of the day."

At this comment, all the skeletons took a big step backward, and their jaws fell open. Some of them even covered up their mouths with their hands in a look of horror. How could anyone say something so cruel? Two of the skeletons in the front were so upset that when their jaws dropped open, they pulled them off and threw them directly at Jrasta. Jrasta took them both in the face and hollered back, "That was like being kissed by a skeleton with no lips!" That one seemed to need a little more work, and the skeletons began to advance again.

By this time, Liam had come up with a couple he thought he could pull off. He ran up to the closest one and yelled, "You need to eat more! You're looking a little thin right here!" He then stabbed it right through where its belly might have been.

The skeleton reacted immediately, and its eyes grew large. Actually, its eyes stayed exactly the same size which was already large. It then seemed to send out a silent scream and collapsed on the spot.

The rest watched this whole experience with awe at Liam's creativity and ran up shouting the same kinds of things. "You need to eat more!" "You appear to be a little thin!" "I think I can see your bones!"

Skeleton after skeleton collapsed before them, but not without a great deal of effort. By the time they had fought their way to the other side of the rocky ridge, they were nearly out of breath, and there were still hundreds of skeletons, all of which moved toward their position. They backed the horses up till they were just on the edge of the rocky ridge before the sand started again. One by one they climbed up into the saddle while the others covered for them. By the end, they could fight from the saddle while the last of them mounted and prepared to go. With that, they finally were able to turn away and head off into the sand again.

"That wasn't so bad!" Jrasta announced while everyone wiped the sweat off their brows and tried to catch their breath. Liam thought it had actually been quite bad. A fight with skeletons was kind of nightmarish.

Jrasta, however, appeared quite pleased with himself. "Just a short trip and we'll be at Kenny the Dragon's lair! We can get the key and then head back home!"

Liam was happy to see the end of the desert up ahead. It ended with a large river which they were able to wade across with the horses. They set up camp on the other side and settled down for supper. Everyone went for a bit of a swim after they ate. They were so excited about a swim, they refused to wait a full hour after eating before they jumped in.

That night, after they sparred for a bit with their swords and with hand-to-hand combat, they all settled down. Liam couldn't get the next day's mission out of his mind. He dreaded going after Kenny the Dragon and hoped they were right. He hoped the name was just a name and didn't actually mean he was a dragon.

19. Kenny

The next morning came early. Liam suspected that it came at the same time as the day before, but the night had passed too quickly, and he was quite tired in the morning. They packed up camp and loaded up without too much talk. It seemed everyone was a little worried about what was to come.

Jrasta had woken up a little earlier than the rest of them and gone out scouting that morning. They didn't know exactly where the path was since they had not traveled in a perfectly straight line across the desert. While out searching, Jrasta had located the path a little way to the south of their position.

The journey to the path was quite nice. There seemed to be a cool breeze coming from the north along the river, and it was very refreshing as they traveled south.

The ground was covered with a thick grass and was quite flat along this way with the occasional tree growing near the river's edge.

The difference between this side of the river and the desert side was remarkable. There even seemed to be some wildlife here as well. Liam saw some families of deer and even wild horses.

After about half an hour, they came across the path and turned onto it. It was sad to leave the river behind, but the cool breeze continued, and the way forward was quite relaxing. They came across some fruit trees and stopped by them for lunch. The fruit seemed like a cross between an orange and a pineapple in flavor but came in the shape of a purple banana with a peel and all.

They didn't stop long at the fruit trees but made sure they got moving again quickly. Now that they were this close to finding the key, they wanted to get on with it, even though they were all a little tense.

Not far from the fruit trees, Jrasta reined up by a large rock. He announced they had arrived, although neither Liam nor Ezra could see anything up ahead. They tied off their horses on some trees nearby and left most of their supplies behind, taking only their weapons, some water and a small snack. They set out over the last little bit on foot, and within a few minutes, Liam could see where they were heading. It was a pit. It was simply a large hole in the ground. It was about the size of his classroom at school, but entirely without any sign or marker to show that it was there. If someone was riding their horse hard, they might not see the pit ahead of them till it was too late.

When they arrived at the edge of the pit, Liam saw a set of stairs following around the outside edge of the pit and leading down into the darkness. Without a word, Jrasta started down.

The stairs were carved right out of the rock on the side of the pit and were slightly damp and slippery. Liam steadied himself on the side wall as he made his way down. As they continued their descent, the light grew dimmer, and the temperature dropped till Liam felt himself shivering from the cold. Everyone moved in silence as they listened intently for Kenny the Dragon… who might not be a dragon.

Liam was still irritated by that one. He really didn't want to battle a dragon, but at the same time, he really wanted Kenny to be a dragon so he could show everyone how silly it was to think someone named "Kenny the Dragon" would not be a dragon.

When they reached the bottom of the pit, Liam looked up to see the entrance far above. From this depth, it now appeared to be not much more than a tiny hole. They had come down quite a distance.

The room they found themselves in at the bottom of the stairs was round, like the pit. There was only one exit. It was directly across from the last step leading into a passageway, and there was a soft glow coming from that direction. They quietly made their way forward, listening closely for any sound that might signal danger.

The passageway was as straight as could be, traveling at a downward angle with the soft glow coming from far ahead. The light grew brighter as they moved along and in time they could see the passageway turn sharply into a well-lit area. They approached the corner, and each one peered around.

The passageway opened up into a large chamber. There were fires burning in little alcoves around the edge of the room giving light. In the center was a large pile of grass and sticks which looked like a large nest or bed of some sort. The ceiling was quite high, and there were some large bats hanging from little cracks and crevices. On the far side of the room was a large opening. If Kenny were, in fact, a large dragon, he would have to use the large opening. There was no sign of Kenny… whether he was a dragon or not.

They stepped into the room and spread out a little bit. Liam wondered if they could simply find the key and get out of there before Kenny showed up, but he didn't think it would be that easy.

As they started making their way around the chamber, a loud growl reverberated through the place. Out of the large opening, a scaly head appeared. The head had large eyes, the size of softballs and two horns on top. He was a dark gray color and, as the Regent had explained, covered in scales. Smoke curled up slowly from his nostrils. As he moved into the room and they saw more of him, they were each filled with dread, all except Jep who appeared bored with the whole situation and was stifling a yawn while eyeing Liam's nose.

The head was attached to a long neck, as large around as the head. As he moved, the neck slowly moved back and forth as if it were slithering like a snake. As his body entered the cavern, they saw he walked on all fours, with a large, solid, muscular body and legs like tree trunks. On his back were two large wings. The tail, like the neck, seemed to slither. Another loud growl erupted from Kenny's throat.

Kenny the Dragon was, in fact, a dragon.

Liam looked over at Jrasta with an expression that said, "See? He is a dragon!"

Jrasta instantly knew what Liam was thinking. He looked back and said, "Well, of course! NOW we can see that he is a dragon!"

They each drew their swords and Jrasta motioned for Liam to step forward. "This is your quest, Liam. Speak up."

Liam stepped forward and swallowed hard. His mouth was suddenly quite dry. "Listen up, Kenny the Dragon! We are here to take back what you stole from the King's Palace. We are after the key. You can either cooperate and give us back the key willingly, or we will take it by force!"

Liam was quite proud of that little speech. It was spur of the moment, but he had tried to sound confident and as if he were speaking with authority. As he spoke, Kenny's unblinking eyes watched him closely, and when finished, silence filled the room.

When Kenny spoke, Liam was quite shocked. He had a high pitched, whiny voice and spoke with a terrible lisp. "But I don't waaaaaaaana give you back the key! Ith miiiiiiiiiiine. I thtole it fair and thquare. I won't give it back tho you'll have to fight me for it!"

162

Liam and the others stared at the dragon for a moment. Somehow a whiny dragon seemed less threatening, and they had to remind themselves that he was still a dragon.

As they stared at him, Liam saw around the dragon's neck was a thin chain with a tiny key. There was no way they could get through this without fighting Kenny. Ezra saw the same thing at the same time. The boys looked at each other and knew what had to be done. They raised their swords together, each crying out a war-cry at the same time. Liam yelled out, "For Arestana and for the future king!" and Ezra cried out, "I have a stone in my shoe!" Liam thought perhaps Ezra didn't quite understand the concept of a war-cry, but he said it with passion and charged forward with Liam.

Time seemed to slow down, and Liam heard epic music start up in his head. The music made the battle the stuff of legend. Side by side, the boys charged forward. Liam wasn't sure if the rest of his friends were behind them or sitting back and waiting to see how it all played out. As they approached Kenny, he reared up on his hind legs and let out a deep, terrifying roar. He then blew fire into the air, singeing the poor bats above him before coming down on all fours to face the charging boys.

The music played even louder in his mind as he leapt into the air just before reaching Kenny. They each swung back their swords for the attack. Ezra brought his sword down on Kenny's neck while Liam thrust his sword into Kenny's chest.

Neither sword did much of anything to the dragon. Each boy landed on the ground, rolling to a stop on either side of Kenny. They had accomplished nothing other than to get Kenny angry, but the music was still playing so they knew the battle was still on. Liam slid under the dragon in the hopes his belly was less protected, and Ezra took another swing, but this time at a leg. Both boys were unsuccessful and had to jump out of the way as Kenny swung his tail in a circle in an attempt to knock them down.

The tail missed Ezra completely, but caught Liam's right arm, knocking the sword clean out of his hand. It flew across the room. They could hear a couple people cheer and looked back to see their friends had found a place to sit and were just enjoying the show.

Liam pulled out his knife and threw it at Kenny's side. He hoped to do at least a little damage, but once again the attack just bounced off the dragon's scales.

As Ezra charged Kenny for another attack, the dragon whipped his head around and grabbed Ezra in his mouth. He tossed him aside. Ezra rolled for a bit on the ground and then came to a stop. At first, there was no movement at all and Liam feared the worst, but then he heard a little groan come from Ezra's direction. At least Ezra was alive.

The dragon turned his attention to Liam and brought his head around to stare him in the eye. Liam knew that if Kenny decided to blow fire at that moment, he would be a goner. Kenny opened his mouth a little to show large, sharp teeth and let out a high pitched giggle before speaking again in his whiny voice. "You are tho dead, little tholdier man. I am tho going to have you for a thnack."

Liam glanced over at his friends, who by this point were eating something that looked a little like popcorn. He knew he would find no help from them.

He realized he needed to come up with some kind of weapon or some way to defeat this dragon. If he didn't, this would be the end. Once he was gone, Ezra might be next and who knew what might happen to his friends. As unconcerned as they seemed, perhaps Kenny would attack them as well.

Kenny came in close so Liam could smell his breath. Obviously, this time of day was morning for Kenny. There was drool dripping from the sides of his mouth, and his eyes seemed to glow like fire. His eyes… that was it! Liam took his finger and poked it as hard as he could into Kenny's eye. Liam knew that no one liked that kind of thing, not even a dragon.

Kenny once again reared up on his hind legs, but this time in pain. "Owthy! That hurth tho much. You boyth are mean to me!" With that, he turned around and bounded back into the cave through which he had originally come.

Liam rushed over to his friend. Ezra wasn't moving and was curled up with his face toward the ground. Liam grabbed his shoulder and rolled him back to see a look of pain on his face. "I think I broke a nail," Ezra moaned. He held it up for Liam and Liam confirmed that his friend had, in fact, broken a nail.

"That looks painful," Liam said, without much emotion. "We need to go after Kenny to get the key." The sound of Kenny's pathetic crying was getting fainter as he ran away from the cavern.

"Why don't we just use this key?" Ezra smiled as he used his uninjured hand to hold up the key they had been looking for. "When I tried to chop off Kenny's head, I happened to hit the chain, and the key fell to the ground. I grabbed it before he threw me over here."

Liam laughed and grabbed the key from his friend. Standing up he yelled to the others, "We have it! We have the key! We can go back to the castle, and I can go home!"

"Not so fast."

Everyone jumped as they heard the voice. They turned to see twelve guards standing in the cave which Kenny had used only a moment before. It was the soldiers from the castle. They still wore their armor, but they were covered in mud and looked quite upset. Obviously, the River Road hadn't worked out well for them.

"We'll take that key, now, if you don't mind." Sergeant Dimmock held out his hand while the other eleven guards drew their swords.

Liam thought this one through. They might be able to defeat the guards a second time, but Ezra was injured, if only slightly, and didn't appear to be able to do much of anything short of lay there and weep. Liam slowly walked over to retrieve his sword and knife, before wandering back to Ezra. He knelt down beside his friend and asked, "Can you run? Is your broken nail going to stop your feet from working?"

"Liam, you're so thoughtful and caring."

Liam rolled his eyes.

Ezra groaned before continuing, "I can run. If you help me up."

Liam pulled his friend to his feet while the guards continued to watch them closely. Liam knew he needed to communicate his plan to the rest of the team. The plan was simple. He wanted everyone to run for the exit. He decided the best way to let everyone know this was his plan was to yell, "RUN!!"

Everyone made for the small passageway through which they had entered. Once there, their eyes had to adjust to the dark, but they knew the guards would have the same problem. They ran as fast as they could toward the pit and charged up the stairs. If they could get to their horses, it would give them a head start. The guards' horses would likely be at the other entrance, quite a ways from the pit. Since they had obviously come through the same entrance Kenny had used, they might even have to contend with a grumpy dragon to get to their horses.

They ran up the stairs, round and round. The stairs seemed even more wet and slippery going up than they had coming down. They ran hard and could hear the guards coming up the stairs as well. About fifty steps up, they encountered a problem they were not expecting. Climbing stairs was exhausting. They had to stop and hold the wall while they gasped for air.

The guards continued to climb and had just about reached them when they themselves had to stop to catch their breath. Liam, Ezra, and the others started to climb again, but this time without as much energy. They looked back to see the guards having a tough time as well.

"Hold on... hold on..." Sergeant Dimmock gasped. "We aren't used to climbing stairs."

"No... we're not going to... let you... catch us..." Liam gasped back.

They all started running again and managed to make it another six steps before having to stop again to catch their breath. Each step was agony, and their legs felt like jelly.

As they started moving again, Jrasta slipped and began to roll back. DOHNK, the only one of their group behind the old man, managed to leap over top of Jrasta's rolling body as he sped down the stairs. He hit the twelve guards with the sound of a bowling ball hitting pins, and all of them started to roll as well.

"Go on without me! Save yourselves!" Jrasta hollered as he rolled.

They all watched in horror as Jrasta disappeared down the steps into the darkness. Liam started to go after him, but DOHNK grabbed his arm. "We have to go." Tears welled up in her eyes as she looked down into the darkness where her friend had disappeared. "We have to leave him. We must get this key back to the castle."

Liam felt a pang of guilt in his heart at the thought of leaving Jrasta behind but knew she was right. They turned back to their climb but continued to have to stop every six or seven steps to catch their breath. In time, they managed to get to the top and went straight for the horses.

They climbed up into their saddles just as the soldiers emerged from the pit. Liam and the others untied Jrasta's horse, and Jep hopped up on the saddle. DOHNK held the reins while they galloped away. No one spoke as they retraced their steps. They couldn't believe they had left Jrasta behind, but it was what he had wanted.

167

20. Kraken

The journey back to the river at the edge of the Sandy Desert was quiet. Liam thought of Jrasta and wondered what fate remained for him. Would the soldiers do him harm? Would he get away? Was he in danger from Kenny the Dragon? Would he manage to get back to Kings-Home on foot?

He kept replaying the whole incident in his mind. He even wondered if they should have left Jrasta's horse behind. He knew that would have been foolish. One of the soldiers simply would have taken it.

Only Jep seemed to be happy. It might have had something to do with the unobstructed view from the back of Jrasta's horse now that there was no one in the saddle in front of him.

They broke for a late supper when they reached the river. As they set up camp, Liam realized it was a lot more work without their friend and mentor. There were, of course, some things Liam didn't appreciate about Jrasta. He tended to make conversations quite difficult. He had an odor about him that was a little hard to handle. He snored… not just a little bit, but he snored like there was something seriously wrong with his nose. Liam remembered the hours he and Ezra had spent not being able to fall asleep because of the terrible noise coming from that man's sinuses. Despite all these things, it was clear they all missed Jrasta.

Finally, Jep gave them a look, and they realized they needed to pull themselves together. Jrasta may not be with them anymore, but he was a strong fellow, and he would make it through. They had a quest, and they needed to focus.

That night after supper, they sparred again with swords and hand to hand combat. Liam and Ezra were getting to the point where they could, for the most part, hold their own against DOHNK. Ezra even managed to disarm her a few times.

When they awoke the next morning, they were about to cross the river and head back through the Sandy Desert when DOHNK made a suggestion. They pulled out Jrasta's map and found Kenny's pit, the Desert, the jungle and approximately where they were. DOHNK wondered if they should avoid the path they'd taken to get there and follow the small river south to where it joined up with the Achtor River. She told them that the river flowed west back toward Kings-Home, and they might be able to gain passage on a boat. That detour could save them days of travel.

It sounded like a good idea, and the group turned south immediately. The Achtor River wasn't far, and by the time they broke for lunch, they could see the water in the distance.

By late afternoon, they were approaching the water's edge where they came upon a small town with a harbor. The people were wary of strangers coming from inland, and they found the people unfriendly. Most of the town's visitors came by boat and stayed on the boats. The people didn't appear to trust anyone from outside.

They called this place Sandyport after the desert a short distance away.

They made their way straight to the docks and found a ship large enough to take all four of them and their horses. The ship was a merchant vessel which sold material and furs from upriver.

They set sail the very next morning. There was a strong wind coming from the east, and they made good time heading west. The captain of the ship, a short, round hairy man with a hook for a foot and a peg for an arm was quite friendly and seemed to enjoy their company. He asked all about their travels, and they told him just about everything, except of course that they were on a quest and had the key to the King's Chest in Liam's pocket. They weren't sure who to trust and thought it was better to keep this detail secret.

The trip back was uneventful the first day, but their situation changed on the morning of the second day. They were lazing around on the deck, chatting with some of the sailors, when the boat lurched to the side. DOHNK was sitting on the rail at that moment, and if it wasn't for Liam grabbing her arm, she would have toppled right into the water.

The captain burst out of his quarters and began giving orders. The sailors rushed around to obey. They fully raised the sails and tied everything down. They also made sure the horses were secure in the hold below and they told their passengers to stay close to the mast. With the sails at full, the ship picked up speed in the water.

When all the orders had been followed, everyone stopped and waited. Liam started to ask what had happened, but the Captain just held up his hand for him to be quiet.

The boat lurched again, but this time everyone except two of the most seasoned sailors were knocked over. Within seconds another more violent lurch happened, and then the boat started to creak like it was about to break apart.

Everyone looked around in fear for a few silent moments before the captain hollered, "It's the Kraken!"

Everyone started to scream at the same time, and DOHNK pulled out her sword. She looked at Liam and Ezra and saw their confused looks. She explained, "The Kraken is a sea monster. It only attacks now and then, but few survive when it goes after a ship. The captain raised the sails to try to outrun it, but it looks like it's targeted us!"

The ship continued to pick up speed. Liam wondered if this would be fast enough to outrun the Kraken, but then he saw the shadows under the water. The creature clearly had no trouble keeping up with them. He could see a dark form circling the ship, even at these speeds.

The water off to the side started to foam, and they could see the monster was about to surface. Men screamed again, and the captain began to weep. The despair could almost be felt across the deck of the boat. The body of the Kraken could clearly be seen under the water, surrounding the ship. The captain called for the men to furl the sails and drop anchor. They couldn't outrun the beast. With the Kraken surrounding the ship, they needed to come to a halt so the hull would not break apart on the body of the giant sea monster.

The Kraken broke the surface and rose up beside the ship. Four of the sailors fainted, and the captain fell to his knees and started biting his nails.

Liam looked at the beast in awe. He looked at its face, its neck, its eyes, the body that stuck up out of the water, the mouth. It was, by far, without a doubt, the most adorable creature he had ever laid his eyes on. If it were small, he would not have been able to resist wrapping his arms around it and giving it a big hug. He had never seen such cute eyes. They were like the eyes of a kitten, times one hundred. Its smile put Liam's heart at ease, and its furry neck and body seemed soft and comforting. Even its sharp teeth seemed friendly. From beside him, he heard Ezra say, "Ahhhhh" and could tell he wasn't the only one taken by the cuteness of this creature.

Liam walked to the edge of the ship and hollered out. "Hello there, wittle guy. Are you wost? Did you wose your mommy?" He was finding the urge to give it a hug almost unbearable. The beast roared as vicious a roar as Liam had ever heard, but at the same time, even the roar was adorable. It was like Liam's three-year-old nephew who liked to pretend he was a tyrannosaurus rex. Sure he was supposed to be dangerous, but when a toddler walks around pretending to be a dinosaur, it's just cute.

At the same time, Liam knew he should not mess with this beast. Though it truly was adorable, it was a dangerous creature, and he needed to give it some space.

He just couldn't stop himself. "Does the wittle Kwaken have something in its thwoat?" Liam asked. He was having trouble not treating it like a baby. He wasn't sure if this was the wisest move, but the Kraken was just so adorable he couldn't help himself.

The beast appeared to become more agitated each time Liam spoke, but there was just no way to stop. "What's a matter, wittle Kwaken? Do you have a booboo?"

The Kraken seemed beside itself with anger. It looked like it didn't know how to respond, but it knew it didn't like this. It began to shake its head back and forth and roar its adorable little roar with even more ferocity. The entire crew and Liam's whole team motioned toward him to try to get him to stop the baby talk. Liam could see how this was a problem and wished he could stop, but it was like he was watching himself through someone else's eyes. The words just flowed out of his mouth.

Liam stepped up on the railing, balanced himself and stretched out his arms before the great beast. He realized he had come too far to turn back now. It was time to bring this hug in for a landing. "Come here, wittle guy. It's time for some wovin'."

The Kraken began to shake. Its eyes flashed red (an adorable red), and it showed all its teeth. Although Liam was taken by the monster's cuteness, he could tell he had crossed the line long before this point and the beast was likely more enraged now than it had ever been in its entire life. It started to flap the little fins which ran down each side of its snake-like body and even the captain of the ship, convinced his life was minutes from coming to an end, let out a little squeak at the cuteness of those fins.

When the rage had reached a peak and Liam, still balanced on the side rails of the boat, thought it was all over, and he was about to die the death of cuteness, a large tear formed in the eye of the Kraken. It started to cry. Not a little sniffle, but a loud, wailing sort of cry. It wept, and tears fell. The tears made huge splashes in the Achtor River. The Kraken was clearly a lonely creature, and this was perhaps the first time anyone had ever shown any affection toward him. He leaned in, and Liam wrapped his arms around the beast's neck, and the two of them wept together.

After a long while, the Kraken pulled back and began to weep even harder. Liam stepped back onto the deck of the boat. The weeping had reached a new level which involved snot and an unfortunate amount of drool. The cries began to come in loud, sobbing bursts. The beast, as cute as it had been while angry, was clearly an ugly crier.

Liam started to gag a little bit, and the entire crew began to feel uncomfortable. The beast just kept on crying, and chunks of snot were getting on the deck. It then leaned in and blew its nose on the front sail.

This was too much for the captain. He looked at the sails and began to gag. Between gags, he called for the anchor to be raised and the sails to be put up. The ship lurched forward. The Kraken still wept, but its body no longer surrounded the ship. They moved on, thankful to be alive.

While the rest of their journey on the river was less life-threatening, it was certainly irritating. As they neared the port at which they planned to disembark, a school of flying fish passed by the boat. The crew could see them coming from a ways off and warned Liam and his friends.

The flying fish would leap out of the water, fly for a short distance and splash back down again. When they arrived at the boat, most of the fish slammed hard into the side of the hull. Liam went to the side of the boat to look over and watched as the fish hit the boat, landed back in the water, shook their heads and tried again with the same result.

The fish that missed the side of the boat, however, were far worse. They moved so fast you couldn't see them coming. Liam and Ezra would be standing on the deck, minding their own business, when a rather large fish would fly up and slap them each in the face. After the first such experience, Liam stood up and tried to see who had hit him, just as another fish came, this one catching him in the stomach and landing on the deck. It flopped its way across the deck and flipped itself into the water. Liam kept low after this, but he was sure the fish were actually trying to hit him. Some would fly just over his head, and as he ducked, they would swing their tail down just a little bit, enough to slap the top of his head. He thought he could hear the fish laughing as they continued on their way.

When the danger seemed to have passed, Liam and Ezra both rose to their feet, sore and a little angry. They looked at each other and started to laugh. They were glad this trial was over as well. They didn't see the one final flying fish leap out of the water, over the rail of the ship, flying right between them. As it passed the boys, it stretched out its fins, one on either side, and smacked each boy before it let out a little fish giggle and slipped back into the water on the other side of the boat.

About an hour later, they pulled into the port. Once they had docked, Liam, Ezra, DOHNK and Jep led their horses up from below and out onto the dock. They thanked the captain for his help. He smiled and offered his help again for the future. They could see he was trying to avoid looking at his sail. The giant Kraken tissue had dried but was no less disgusting now than when it was fresh. He thanked Liam, however, for his ingenious reaction to the beast. He told Liam that his kindness to the Kraken had saved their lives and he would always be welcome back on his ship.

The town they had landed in was a little larger than Sandyport. It was named Whiteridge after the limestone rock all along the shore. The people here were friendly, and they stayed the night at an inn on the edge of town. The next day, they rose early and continued their journey.

21. Harv Again

Jrasta's map was proving to be quite a help on their journey.

As they left Whiteridge, they examined the map to see that the path back to Kings-Home wasn't far. They just needed to head north a little ways from the town to find their way. The road from the Achtor River wound up through the hill, getting smaller and smaller till it had nearly disappeared before it connected up with the path running to Kings-Home. They turned west and started for home.

They were getting used to traveling without Jrasta, although every stop for a meal, every look at the map, every time they wondered what to do next they were reminded of his absence. Fortunately, DOHNK was pretty good at thinking on her feet, and Jep was able to look at them now and then to give them some much needed advice.

When they reached the path, Liam was surprised to see that he didn't recognize it at all. "I don't remember traveling along this part of the path."

Ezra looked concerned till DOHNK reminded them they had left the path shortly after Harv's house to go to the Lizard Men Village. In a short while, they crested a hill and saw a familiar looking house up ahead. From the smoke trailing up out of the chimney, Harv was clearly at home.

Liam's first thought was to keep on going. "We've bothered him enough. Let's leave him alone and camp up the road a little bit."

Ezra, DOHNK and Jep all disagreed. DOHNK explained, "Harv and Jrasta are pretty close. Harv will want to know what happened to his friend. We have to tell him. Besides, Harv will want to give us all a warm bed and a hot meal since we're Jrasta's friends."

Liam wasn't sure about that. He hoped he could help them see reason since Jrasta wasn't there to add a certain degree of irrationality to the conversation. He thought he would try to help them understand. "Were the rest of you not there when we stopped in on the way through this area? Didn't you see how much Harv despised Jrasta? He even turned him over to the Lizard Men! Harv doesn't care about Jrasta! He hates him!" Liam felt bewildered at how anyone could not see the obvious disgust Harv had for Jrasta.

Ezra, DOHNK and Jep just ignored Liam, and when they arrived, they went around to the back. They stabled the horses and made their way to the front door. They knocked, and the door opened almost immediately. When Harv saw them, his face lit up. "DOHNK, Ezra, Liam, Jep! It's great to see you! Did you finish your quest? Wait, what am I doing? Come in, come in!" He grabbed each of them by the arm and pulled them inside.

Once they were in, Harv led them into the sitting room to warm by the fire, and he busied himself in the kitchen, making some tea. He hummed to himself while he ran back and forth between the kitchen and pantry. Liam was pleased to hear someone who could sing. He had grown to love every one of his friends in Arestana, but none of them could carry a tune to save their lives.

He was fine with this. He made it a point to not look down on people just because they couldn't sing, but he wished they would recognize their inability and perhaps sing less.

After about twenty minutes, Harv came into the room with tea, cookies, bread and fresh fruit. He made sure they all had enough and then sat down with a big smile on his face. Liam wasn't entirely sure if this was the same Harv. When they were here a short while ago, he was cranky and seemed to cry a lot. This man was happy!

"Tell me everything! I assumed you rescued Jrasta, but I don't see him here. Is that old guy still stuck with the Lizard Men?" Harv chuckled at that thought. "He'll be pretty grumpy after being stuck in a cage this long."

They all looked at Liam, and he started to tell the tale. He told how they had rescued Jrasta from the Lizard Men, then made their way through the Dark Jungle. He told how they had survived the man-eaters and the fortress. He told him about Mary and all about the Sandy Desert. He shared about finding Kenny's pit and that Kenny was, in fact, a dragon. Harv seemed especially surprised at that news.

Harv listened intently, asking the odd question here and there about the journey. He seemed to enjoy hearing the tale and offered many compliments on their bravery and determination. When Liam came to the point where Jrasta rolled down the stairs, Harv's whole body tensed.

"He said, 'Go on without me! Save yourselves!'?" Harv asked. "Then he simply rolled down the stairs?"

"Yes. It was hard to leave him behind, but we decided to honor his request. We hope he made it out alive." Ezra explained. No one was making eye contact with anyone at this point. They were all ashamed of running and fearful for Jrasta's safety.

Harv stood up and brought himself to his full height. Seeing as he was quite a short, thin man, this was like when a child tries to look tall. "Why would you leave him behind??? He obviously wanted you to come after him!"

For once, Liam wasn't the only one confused. "But he told us to go on without him! To save ourselves! He obviously wanted us to leave!" Liam looked at the others who nodded in agreement.

"No, no, no, no, no! When he said, 'go on without me,' he meant, 'don't leave me here with the soldiers, they're so boring!' Don't you know that the Regent's guards are so incredibly boring? They'll take him with them and tell him boring stories about boring adventures they wished they had. They'll tell him about how they boringly arrested some poor guy for stealing, only to find out they boringly got the wrong guy, how they have to stand for hours guarding boring doors that lead to empty, boring rooms. They are just so boring!" Harv looked close to panicking. "This is not good. This is bad. Poor Jrasta! This is not good."

Harv ran out of the room at this point while Liam yelled out, "I thought you didn't like Jrasta?"

Harv stopped and turned around. His face went red, and his voice raised about two octaves. "Don't like Jrasta???" He squeaked. "You think I don't like Jrasta?" His whole body was shaking with rage. "Jrasta is my closest friend! We are practically brothers! I would do anything for Jrasta!"

With that Harv turned around and ran out the door. He slammed it behind himself and was gone.

"Well, we read that one wrong." Ezra declared. "I guess we'll have to remember in the future that 'Go on without me! Save yourselves!' means, 'Don't go on without me, come and save me!'"

"Guess so," DOHNK said, going back to the cookies and tea.

Harv didn't return before bedtime, so they hit the sack without him.

The next morning, Harv still wasn't back. Liam wondered what could be keeping the poor man, but after breakfast, they knew they had to continue on their way. They went around back and saddled the horses. They led their mounts out front, and as they were about to head out, Harv returned along with Jrasta.

"You found him!" Ezra declared.

"Of course I found him! I just had to find the group of guards, subdue them and get away while they were figuring out how to react. They aren't the brightest group of people in the world."

With that, Harv turned to Jrasta, pushed him off the horse and screamed, "Get away from me!"

Jrasta hit the ground hard and got up laughing. He said, "You're such a kidder, Harv!" as he reached up and pulled what looked like Harv's wallet from the man's back pocket.

Liam decided he no longer cared what was going on between Harv and Jrasta. He simply handed the reins of Jrasta's horse over to him, and the older man climbed up. "Well," said Jrasta, "we won't get back to Kings-Home standing here. Let's ride!"

They waved goodbye to Harv as they continued on their journey. While they rode, Jrasta explained a little bit about what had happened to him. He started by sharing how disturbed he was that they were so willing to go on without him. He didn't feel anyone should ever abandon a friend and simply try to save themselves. He then shared that the guards had captured him and forced him to listen to their boring stories while they rode back. At this point, Jrasta went on for a while sharing boring stories about being told boring stories. He told them the guards were nearly to Harv's house when his friend showed up, overpowered all twelve guards, cut the rope holding Jrasta and brought him back.

Liam struggled to picture Harv overpowering twelve guards single-handedly. Harv didn't seem like a fighter. However, since not much in this world made sense, this was the least of his worries. Regardless of what happened, it was good to have Jrasta back.

The journey leading back to Kings-Home led them first through Booger Bully territory. It was just as gross as Liam remembered. Large globs of snot hung from branches and bushes. It was disgusting. They led their horses around the slimy patches and managed to avoid most of them.

Once again, they tried to move through this section of the path as quietly as they could. Liam didn't know where the actual Booger Bully village was, but he hoped it was a long ways away. He didn't like the thought of having to fight them again. It wasn't that he was afraid of them. He was actually quite confident he could hold his own against them now with all the training and experience he had, and he knew together they could defeat the Booger Bullies a second time without difficulty. It was that he found the whole "snot thing" quite gross. He had had enough gag-worthy experiences this trip.

For a while, everything was fine till they heard some noise up ahead. Just a short distance away, the path curved sharply to the left and it sounded like a crowd was coming toward them from around the corner. Jrasta motioned them off the path and into the forest. They managed to get behind some trees in just the nick of time as a large group of noses appeared, followed by their owners. When they had passed by Liam and the others, they heard more Booger Bullies coming and stayed where they were, waiting for the danger to pass. After this group, a few more appeared, then more.

This went on for a while, and eventually, they realized they could be waiting a long time as the group of noses with people attached passed by. It appeared as though this was their afternoon walk along the path. Jrasta motioned for all of them to quietly make their way deeper into the forest. He explained it would be best to travel through the woods for a little ways in the hopes of getting by the walking snot-makers.

After quietly moving through the trees, they managed to get to a point where they could no longer see the road. They stopped briefly for something to eat, hoping that they were a safe distance from the path, then started moving along parallel with the path again. It was much slower to move through the forest than on the path as they needed to move quietly in the forest and navigate around trees and various obstacles.

As they snuck through the woods, they came across a small hill standing in their way. Jrasta suggested they go around to the right to help keep them away from the path and the Booger Bullies. As they made their way around the hill, the ground dropped off, leaving only a small ledge just barely large enough for the horses to walk along. Liam took the lead and started inching his way around. The rest of the team had encouraged Liam to take the lead on this one as they felt it was best if he risked his life first so they could see if it was safe for the rest of the group.

When they were just about the entire way around the hill, with only a step or two to go, Liam's foot landed on a rather large and surprisingly slippery glob of snot. The first thing he realized was that he was about to fall. The second thing he realized was that it would hurt a lot.

Fortunately for him, he was wrong... about the second thing. It didn't actually hurt much. There was so much snot that his fall was cushioned and he simply slid down the entire way. There was really very little pain.

Sadly, he was absolutely correct about the first thing. He did fall, and he fell fast. He fell so fast, in fact, that he could not see or make sense of anything as he slid and spun on his way down. He couldn't even hear his friends gasping out in terror for Liam and relief for themselves that Liam had fallen and not them.

When he finally stopped sliding, he had to take a moment to get his bearings. He looked around and up, hoping to see his friends, but could not actually see the hill he had been climbing around. In fact, there was no hill for quite a distance. As he looked at the line of snot behind him, the truth dawned on him. He had slid much, much farther than he would have expected. He could see the hill, and he could just barely make out his friends off in the distance.

Liam stood up and tried to wipe the snot off his clothing. As he finished getting the bulk of it off, he was hit from behind by a flying chunk of booger. His feet left the ground, and the force of the snot slammed him into a tree, sticking him to the trunk. He struggled to get free or even to get to his sword, but to no avail.

He looked up to see eight Booger Bullies emerge from behind the trees. They came upon him and removed his sword from its sheath as well as his knife. Within moments, he was not only pulled down from the tree but also securely tied up in what looked like a somewhat more stringy form of snot.

His heart was pounding hard as he realized what was about to come. They were going to force him to eat the Snot Root and turn him into a Booger Bully. He struggled, but with no success.

The trip to their village was different than he'd expected. He had planned on resisting the entire way, but the Booger Bullies slid to their village, more than walked there. All his resisting did little to nothing as they slid along.

Once there, they took him to the center of the village and brought out the Snot Root. It looked disgusting, but what surprised him was the smell. It smelled good, really good. He even started salivating a lot. He found he wanted it. It smelled like bacon and french fries, or more like deep fried panzerotti. Maybe it smelled like chips and dip.

He decided it didn't matter what it smelled like. He would resist! He would hold out and refuse to allow them to force it into him. His friends would come for him, and he just had to hold out till then. It smelled so good, but he would clamp his teeth down tight, hold his lips closed and nothing would get in. He knew he just needed to finish chewing what was in his mouth and swallow and then he could resist.

What was in his mouth? He was shocked to realize that he had eaten the Snot Root willingly. He knew he should spit it out right away, but decided to swallow what he had in his mouth rather than be rude.

Liam realized too late that he shouldn't swallow it. He knew he needed to stop as he raised the Snot Root to his mouth for the fifth bite but just couldn't find the willpower. The only thing that stopped the flow of Snot Root into his mouth was when he was so full, he feared he might throw up.

Liam could see something happening in front of him. Something was growing. It took him a moment or two before he realized it was his nose. He struggled and screamed and swallowed the last bit of tasty Snot Root in his mouth. He didn't want to become like them! He could resist! He was not like them. He just wanted to shoot snot at people and help them to experience the incredible taste of Snot Root.

Liam now had a new mission in life. He would take Snot Root to the world and help everyone to enjoy the wonder and privilege of eating such a wonderful treat. His friends would have to be first. He would find them and help them see how wonderful Snot Root could be for them.

22. Mushrooms

Ezra watched his friend slide down the hill. He was somewhat relieved that Liam had gone first. He knew that he could be the one being carried away on the snot slide. He was also somewhat disappointed. Liam looked like he was having fun. The look of terror on Liam's face along with the speed told him this was the way to go! He decided he would not let Liam be the only one to enjoy snot sliding and jumped forward.

The back of his shirt caught on something, and he felt himself yanked back. He looked over his shoulder to see Jrasta shaking his head. "What do you think you're doing? Look down there and tell me what you see!"

Ezra looked to see Liam, way in the distance, cleaning snot off his shirt. "He's wiping snot off his shirt! Looks like fun!"

"Look at the trees just past where he stopped," Jrasta said.

Ezra scanned the trees, seeing nothing but leaves and bark. "I don't see anything, just a bunch of trees with... whoa!" Ezra saw what Jrasta was talking about. About six Booger Bullies were sneaking up on Liam. Within moments, Liam was captured and being dragged back into the woods.

"We need to go after him!" Ezra declared, feeling frustrated with Jrasta. "I could be down there right now helping him fight off the Booger Dudes!"

"No, Ezra," Jrasta said. "You would have been captured as well. We need to take a different approach if we are to rescue our friend."

They turned back along the ledge and made their way to more solid ground. Getting the horses to walk back along the ledge was far more difficult than one might have thought. They found a place to leave the horses and tied them up, making sure their mounts had enough food and water to carry them through for a time. They found a safe way to climb down the hill, then carefully and quietly moved in the direction they had seen Liam slide.

When they had made some progress through the woods, Jrasta found a small area where they were fairly well covered. They stopped together, and he explained the plan.

"By this point, they have him in their village and are likely feeding him Snot Root. He will be a Booger Bully soon, there's not much we can do about that. However, we might be able to save him and save all the other Booger Bullies. They are not evil, they have just eaten the Snot Root, and it turns them into these large-nosed, snot-flinging monsters. They lose control and attack anyone who comes near, trying to turn them into what they have become."

"It is said there is an antidote," Jrasta explained. "Growing near the Snot Root is a mushroom which counters the effect of the root and is capable of turning the bullies back into people. The village itself is built around the area where the Snot Root grows. If we can find their village, we should be able to find some of these mushrooms!"

Ezra listened intently, excited about the possibility of Liam's rescue. When Jrasta finished, Jep was the first to nod his agreement with the plan and each person followed in turn.

It was getting close to supper time, but Ezra didn't feel like eating. As he looked around at his friends, none of them appeared hungry either. They were clearly all just as worried sick for Liam as he was. He also felt the many boogers all over the bushes and trees didn't help with his appetite.

They made their way through the bushes and trees as they moved in the direction they had seen Liam taken. When they found the spot where he'd been captured, they found a long line of snot which led through the woods. They followed the snot. Ezra hoped it would take them where they needed to go.

Ezra was nearly shaking with excitement. He was scared, for sure, but he loved the idea of another fight with the Booger Bullies and hoped he could take on Liam before he was turned back into a normal human. Liam was his best friend, but he knew the two of them were pretty evenly matched when they would spar each evening. He hoped Liam's extra-large nose would put him at a disadvantage so he could take him down!

The sun was starting to set by the time they came to the village. They could see lights up ahead from fires and torches.

Jrasta split them into two groups to search for the mushroom antidote. He went with DOHNK and Ezra went with Jep. Before they parted ways, Jrasta warned everyone to be careful not to eat the Snot Root. He warned them that it smelled great, but would change them in moments.

They searched the woods for any sign of Snot Root or mushrooms. There was no sign of either at first, but then Ezra started to smell a turkey dinner. It smelled so good! It also smelled like steak and maybe even some of Masha's homemade soup. He couldn't imagine where that smell was coming from out here, but he knew he wanted some!

They crept around a tree and Ezra saw the Snot Plant. It looked like a small tree with seven or eight leafless branches. He could see the occasional root sticking out of the ground and knew the glorious smell was coming from there. If it weren't for Jep giving him a look, he would not have been able to resist.

"Right. Okay. Don't eat the Snot Root. Gotcha!" Ezra said, trying to convince himself. "If the Snot Root is here, the mushrooms should be around here somewhere."

They searched the ground and within moments had found a large patch of mushrooms growing at the base of a tree. By this time, the sun had set, and most of the light they had left was coming through the trees from the village.

Ezra reached down to pick a mushroom. The instant it broke away from the ground, it released a very different smell than the Snot Root. It stunk. Bad. Not a bad smell like socks which had been in a shoe a little too long. Not a bad smell like when an outhouse blows up (Ezra had seen that happen more than once). Not even a bad smell like if you were to run a marathon with no deodorant and covered in pig manure. This was more like all of those together, times six hundred. Maybe worse.

Ezra and Jep both fell over and started puking everywhere. They tried as hard as they could to puke silently, but it turned out Jep was a loud puker. It was as if each upchuck had to be screamed out of his belly.

Ezra quickly grabbed as many of the mushrooms as he could hold in one arm and grabbed the puking poultry in the other. He ran as fast as he could in the direction Jrasta had gone. He hoped they could get together and regroup before the Snot Buckets came for them. From the sounds of the people in the village, he knew they had heard Jep. A glance in the direction of the village told him the Booger Bullies were on their way to investigate the noise.

190

Ezra could hear the sound of puking ahead. Jrasta and DOHNK must have found some mushrooms as well, and they were both clearly as loud as Jep. Within moments he could see them and burst through the bushes to get to them.

Jrasta was on the ground, holding a bunch of mushrooms. In between heaving, he told Ezra to leave the three of them behind and take the mushrooms. "If you... hhhwwuuooo... hide in the woods... haaaahhh... you can sneak into the village tonight... hhhhrrrreeehhh... and throw the mushrooms into the well... bleeeehhhh."

That was all Jrasta seemed to be able to get out. Ezra could feel the adrenaline pumping through his body. This was the kind of thing he lived for! Adventure! Fun! Seeing other people puke! This was a story to be told for generations!

He could barely contain himself, and without thinking, he yelled, "LET'S DO THIS!" and kicked Jep like a football. Jep did not like being kicked, judging by the look he gave Ezra as he soared away. As he flew, he let another puke flow from his mouth with a scream that echoed through the trees.

"I probably shouldn't have done that," Ezra said out loud, before grabbing the mushrooms from Jrasta and disappearing into the bushes. He hid out of sight just in time as the Booger Bullies burst through the trees and came upon Jrasta and DOHNK. Another one walked up carrying Jep. Ezra realized with horror that this last one was wearing Liam's clothes.

He was instantly filled with rage! That monster had stolen his friend's clothing! What would possess a creature to do such a thing? It took Ezra a few moments to figure out it was, in fact, Liam, just with a huge nose.

While Ezra watched from the bushes, they dragged all his friends back to the center of the village. The Booger Bullies tied them up, and Ezra could see DOHNK, Jrasta and Jep all being offered Snot Root. Jep looked the most confident as they all tried to resist, but within seconds even Jep was chewing on something, and his beak seemed a little larger than normal. It wasn't long before all had given in to the temptation and become Booger Bullies.

Ezra realized he was their only hope. He couldn't be careless with this. He had to take his time. He settled down where he was and waited for complete darkness and for the Booger Bullies to go to sleep.

While he waited, he began to think matters through. He wondered if the mushrooms were not only the antidote for someone who had eaten Snot Root, but maybe they could help prevent the Snot Root from working in the first place. He grabbed one and popped it into his mouth thinking it would disgust him beyond measure. He was surprised to find it was sweet. In fact, the moment it touched his tongue the nasty smell seemed to disappear and the mushroom became the best tasting food he had ever eaten!

He pulled his small sack of supplies from his back and emptied the contents onto the ground. He grabbed all the mushrooms and began breaking them up into small pieces and stuffed his sack with them. He watched as the village settled down for the night and the Booger Bullies all went to bed. His friends, by this point, looked just like all the other monsters. The only way to tell them apart (aside from the large-beaked Jep) was by their clothing. Their noses had grown large, and the snot flow had begun.

When the village had quieted down, Ezra left his hiding place. He could see a well just at the edge of the village and made his way toward it through the trees. When it appeared as though most Booger Bullies were settled down for the night and the few who remained awake were not looking, he crept out and emptied the contents of his sack into the well.

He silently moved back toward the forest and found a place with thick bushes to settle down for the night. He would just have to wait this one out.

The next morning, Ezra woke up with the sun. He knew he had to be quiet if he was to remain free. He lifted his head and peeked out over the village. He could see a number of the snot creatures making their way around the huts. A few of them were already at the well and drawing water. They carried bucket after bucket back to the center of the village to a series of tables. A huge pile of Snot Root was laid out on the tables, and the water carriers were filling goblets from the buckets.

When all this was done, they sat down to eat. The Booger Bullies all dug into their Snot Root, drinking the water as they went.

Ezra watched in anticipation as they each finished their breakfast and their water. He worried that perhaps he hadn't put enough mushrooms into the well or maybe somehow it wasn't going to work. He was busy formulating Plan B when he saw one of the Bullies stand up quickly and yell. Something was happening.

The snot monster grabbed his nose and yelled again, this time he appeared to be in pain. Another one followed suit and then another, till every last Booger Bully was holding their nose and screaming. Some fell to the ground, and Ezra noticed their noses were shrinking. He couldn't help himself; he stood up and cheered. None of the bullies noticed as they were all by this point on the ground, writhing in pain.

The whole process of turning back into normal people took about five minutes, although it seemed like hours to Ezra. When it was done, they all looked around in confusion at one another.

Ezra walked out to the crowd and explained to them all what had happened. He took the time to emphasize his heroic role in providing the antidote to each of them. They all gathered around Ezra and thanked him. He repeated the story again of how he had saved the day and informed them he definitely was their hero. He finished up this moment of celebration by encouraging a group-wide cheer for himself.

Liam watched Ezra's expression. His friend now appeared fully satisfied that everyone knew how awesome he was. Ezra did like attention.

Liam signaled to Jrasta who was busy wiping snot off his upper lip. Jrasta understood it was time for him to give some clarity as to the next step. As he wiped the last of the mucus off his face, he hollered out for everyone to stop congratulating Ezra and listen up.

"We need to get all of you back home. We're heading to Kings-Home, and you're welcome to join us if you'd like. It's about a five-day journey, so we'll need lots of supplies. If you're coming with us, gather up any water bottles and any food or items you may wish to take with you. Make sure whatever you bring with you, you can carry for the entire five days. We leave in ten minutes." With that, Jrasta walked to the edge of the village, sat down and immediately began to snore.

The people began to busy themselves around the village, gathering up what few belongings they had. Most of what people owned, aside from the clothes they were wearing, were large handkerchiefs in varying states of use. Most people simply left those behind. They had plenty of water skins and filled these to the brim from the well. As for food, they had little food apart from the Snot Root. Ezra had to stand guard in that area to prevent people from harvesting more for the road back. Fortunately, with the taste of the mushroom in his mouth, he found he was personally not tempted by the wonderful smell coming from the roots.

In short order, the entire village gathered around Jrasta. He stood up, stretched and took off into the woods. After a long hike and climb, they managed to find the horses just where they had left them. Their mounts seemed anxious to get going. Liam and his friends hopped up on the horses and led the people back to the path. Once there, they made surprisingly good time. The men and women from the village were quite excited about leaving their former life behind and getting back to the city. Many of them had left family and friends behind, some even years ago and they longed to be back with them.

The days ahead passed quickly. They were soon back in the territory patrolled by the King's soldiers, or the Regent's soldiers, and the way forward was safe and well-traveled. They were all looking forward to being back home, and Liam was hoping he could return to his own world the moment they handed back the key. He missed being home, and he missed his mom and dad. He even missed school. Or at least he missed lunch-time at school... when Harry wasn't around.

On the afternoon of the fifth day, they arrived at Kings-Home. As they entered the city, the former Booger Bullies turned to Liam, Ezra and the others and thanked them for all they had done and then each one left to go their own way.

The five were happy to be back, but as they moved through the streets, they noticed something was not quite right. Where people had before bustled around with smiles on their faces and had chatted freely on the corners, people now moved quickly from doorway to doorway. Few people stayed out on the street for long. As they moved through the marketplace, they were shocked to see that it was empty... not just of people, but of shops. There were no shops at all, just a large open area.

"Before we go to the castle, let's visit Masha. Something's not right here. She can let us in on what's going on." Jrasta led them to a familiar looking doorway. They tied up the horses out front and wandered in.

As Liam stepped through the doorway, he was grabbed by the shirt and dragged far into the room. Whoever had grabbed him let go and he turned around to see a mass of hair with arms dragging the rest of the group in after him. Masha slammed the door shut behind her and glared at each of them.

She looked right at Liam and pointed her finger directly at his nose. "You did this. This is all your fault!"

23. Lockdown

Masha advanced on Liam like she was about to attack. He backed away and found himself bumping up against the wall. Her eyes might have been flashing with anger, but it was hard to tell what was going on underneath those brows.

He remembered that DOHNK was Masha's granddaughter and wondered how DOHNK managed to have such normal eyebrows when her grandma seemed to have an entire head of hair squeezed into those two little spots above her eyes.

Shaking his head to bring himself back to the situation at hand, he decided he'd try to talk his way out of this. "Uhhh... I didn't do nothing'!" Liam wasn't always the best with words.

She grabbed him by the collar and pressed her nose up close to his. Her breath reminded him of the dragon's morning breath he had smelled about a week ago, but Masha's also had a smell of rotten soup to it. The combination made him think this was something from which death itself would flee. He was trying not to gag as she spoke. "I think you planned to do this all along! I think you've conspired with the Regent! I think you're the enemy of Arestana!"

Liam gathered his thoughts together. He didn't know what Masha was talking about, but he knew something bad had happened while they were gone. Someone had done something, and now the whole city was in trouble. He knew from experience with Jrasta that these people saw the world differently than he did and anything he said could have disastrous results. He also knew Masha's breath wasn't getting any better and he was nearing his limits. He had an idea and hoped it would help calm Masha down. "Do you have any soup? I'm hungry!"

Masha's face lit up. She smiled brightly, and Liam was sure if he could see her eyes, he'd see a happy look. "Of course I have soup! Sit down, and I will get you something to eat, you poor, hungry traveler. I bet you've been thinking about my nice warm soup for two weeks now."

She turned and bounded over to the kitchen which was about a step and a half away. Liam sat down along with Ezra and the others. Before he knew what was happening, the soup had been placed before him and Ezra, their tongues had been pinched by some rather dirty fingers, and both their faces were being held down in some surprisingly hot soup. He knew from the last time this had happened that the only way to survive was to finish the soup. Liam was pleasantly surprised to find it tasted rather good.

When they had both finished, Jep stood a fair distance away with his eye on Ezra. He was clearly still a little upset about how Ezra had used him as a towel the last time to clean his face. Liam also noticed Ezra eyeing Jep.

Moving like lightning, Ezra leapt across the table for the chicken. Jep was fast, but in such a small house, there were not many places to hide. Ezra caught the chicken in no time. Liam decided it was time to act a little more Arestanian. Each boy used a different side of Jep to clean off their faces.

While Jep scurried away, Jrasta asked Masha if she could explain what had happened in the city. She leaned back in her chair and eyed each member of the group one by one. At least it appeared she was looking at each one in turn. How she saw through that forest of hair was anyone's guess.

"Shortly after you all left, the Regent started acting a little strange," Masha said this in a scream. Most of the time she spoke, she screamed her words. Liam didn't know why. He wanted to encourage her to be quiet, but at the moment, she did not seem mad at him, and he was hoping to keep it that way.

She continued with the same volume. "He started closing the gates at odd times of the day and arresting people for questioning. He even started searching people's homes. Many people wondered what was going on, but I think he was upset that a traveler had come and been sent on a quest for the key and, if successful, he might lose his authority. If all of you returned, he would have to step down as Regent."

"After about four days of this, he passed a law that said all travelers would be arrested and put to death. Now, this is not the kind of thing we Arestanians are going to put up with! We receive travelers all the time from different worlds, and they do quests. Good quests! It's part of who we are and what we do! I mean, if he wants to execute them after they finish their quest, that would be fine, but not before!"

Liam was disturbed to see each of his friends nod their heads in agreement.

"The people revolted. They came to the castle gates and demanded that the law be changed. The Regent refused and sent his guards out. They arrested many people, put a curfew on the town and shut down the market. The guards aren't happy about this either, but they have to follow orders because he's the Regent."

They listened intently to Masha's quick explanation, and Liam felt guilty. It was because of him that all this was happening. But then again, he hadn't had a choice about coming here in the first place.

"So, if we show up with the key, what will he do?" Liam asked.

Jrasta spoke up in response to this question. "If it's just the Regent and a few of his guards, he will probably throw us in prison and hide the key. But if the people find out that the key has been found and been used on the chest, they will no longer feel they have to listen to the Regent at all. None of his guards, except maybe his closest ones, will listen to him anymore."

Liam knew that this was another moment for a hero to step forward. The people of Kings-Home needed him, and he would answer that need! He stood up, raised his fist in the air and raised his voice to say, "Then we have to get the people to the castle and open that chest!" He felt confident and courageous. He was ready to come to the aid of the people of Kings-Home! He stood there for a moment or two while everyone just stared at him.

DOHNK was the first to speak up, "Why do you have your fist up in the air? Are you going to do something with it?"

"No, it just seemed like the right thing to do." Liam felt his face getting a little red.

"Well, that's odd. I wondered if you were going to do something with it, but you just stood there." Ezra piped in. "I thought maybe you were going to knock on a door with it or start swinging it at us."

"Yes, it was really quite threatening." Masha looked uncomfortable.

"I was just... never mind."

"Right. Sit down, Liam. You're confusing everyone." Jrasta said. "Here's the plan: Masha, I want you to spread the word that at ten o'clock tomorrow morning, everyone in the city is to be at the

South entrance to the castle. There is a balcony on that side which opens to the throne room. We will sneak into the castle, get the chest and drag it to the balcony. At ten o'clock, we will open the chest and announce the new King of Arestana!"

Everyone cheered and raised their fists in the air, all except Liam. They all looked at him like he was being difficult.

They spent the evening resting up. When it was time to sleep, Liam, Ezra and Jrasta spread out on the floor of Masha's cramped house while Masha and DOHNK took the bunks. Jep hid up on a shelf. He still looked somewhat upset at being used as a face wipe. Everyone felt a certain amount of nervousness about the next day, but they knew what had to be done.

The next morning they rose early while it was still dark and had some breakfast before heading out. Masha left well before the rest of the group to start spreading the word.

As they stepped out onto the street, the early morning light was just starting to creep up in the east which still allowed them some darkness to use as cover. They made their way to the castle without much difficulty. There were guards on the occasional corner, but each one was still sound asleep from their night "watch."

When they arrived at the castle, they found the gates closed up tight. Jrasta waved them on to a small door off to the side. It was a solid door and looked to be as much of a barrier as the main gate, but Jrasta knocked on it and waited for a response. A few moments later, a bleary-eyed guard opened the door and looked out at them. "Yah? What do ya want?"

Jrasta charged the man and knocked him back into the guard room. Liam thought it might have been helpful if Jrasta had explained this part of the plan ahead of time so they could be prepared, but he and the others leapt into action without too much of a pause. Liam charged into the room to find three guards trying to hold Jrasta down. He jumped on the guard closest to him and saw that Jep, DOHNK and Ezra attacked as well.

The guards were slow and easily overcome. Within minutes, all the guards were tied up and gagged. Jrasta closed the door and locked it.

There was a small room just off to the side, set into the wall. Jrasta led the group in there, and Liam saw it was a small armory, filled with suits of armor and weapons in the guard's style. Each one suited up. Liam assumed Jrasta's plan involved impersonating guards. Liam's uniform matched Jrasta, DOHNK and Ezra's, while Jep's uniform seemed a little different in style. Liam wondered how it could be that they might have a guard uniform made for a chicken in there, but discarded the question. This was Arestana, after all.

When they walked out of the small side room wearing guard uniforms, they saw one of the guards had worked his gag out of his mouth. He looked at the group and started telling them off. "What? You're all castle guards? Why did you attack us? You could have just come in. You didn't need to tie us up. I'll see that you are all disciplined!"

Liam wondered how this man could be so dense.

The guard continued, "I'll have you before the Regent for this. You'll be in so much trouble you'll…" the man cut off his threat at the sight of Jep. He began to stutter a bit before stumbling through an apology. "I'm… I'm sorry sir. I didn't realize a Captain of the guard was in your party. I would not have questioned anything you or any of your guards had done if I had known. You'll have to forgive me for not saluting. My hands are tied up behind my back, sir."

Jep looked at the man and raised his chin up in the air. He then looked at the man as if to say, "As you were," before walking with Jrasta to the door leading into the courtyard.

The courtyard was fairly empty at this time of day, but there were some guards on the move. They noticed the stable boy busied himself with talk about the horses. "I gots horses. I feeds horses. I gots horses that I feeds. Theys are good horses, but sometimes theys are horses."

No one paid the five of them much attention, except to salute Jep as he walked by. Liam thought with the guard armor, this would be easy! They could simply walk into the throne room and open the chest!

As they were about to enter a wooden doorway to make their way through the castle, the door burst open and a rather large guard with a deep voice stepped out. He bellowed with a voice that Liam thought could be heard clear across the city. "Inspection! Time for Inspection. Form up!"

Guards started spilling out of every doorway and entranceway into the courtyard. They moved toward the center of the courtyard and started forming up in ranks. The large guard looked at Liam and the others and hollered, "Get moving! Inspection!"

Jrasta pushed them over to stand in line, and each tried to mimic the other guards. They stood with their backs straight, their left foot forward a little bit and their right hand, palm upwards like they were holding a serving tray. They each bounced slightly on the spot. Liam thought this was odd in many ways, but also very fitting for this world. He did his best to match the stand and the movement. He felt like he was supposed to start dancing or something and wouldn't have been surprised if some music started and the inspection of the guard turned into a flash mob.

The large guard with the big voice walked along the line of guards, inspecting each one in turn. Liam saw that it wouldn't take long for the man to get to him and his friends. He wasn't sure where Jep had disappeared to.

Two guards away from Liam, the inspection guard started to yell. At first, everything he said was entirely unintelligible, but as he continued to yell, Liam found he could start to make out the occasional word. He was trying to communicate to this guard that his armor was crooked and something about how he would be a better stable boy than a soldier.

When this was finished, the inspection guard moved on. The guard right next to Liam apparently passed with flying colors, but as the inspection guard came upon Liam, his face took on a horrified look. He started to scream, and Liam used his recently obtained interpretive skills to try to understand the insults. Something about how he had never seen such poor care and concern on the part of a soldier before and that he was a disgrace to guards everywhere. Liam was afraid he was about to be thrown out when something caught the inspection guard's eye.

The man looked down and made eye contact with Jep. Immediately he stood up straight and saluted. "I'm sorry, SIR! I didn't realize you were among us. I was just doing our morning inspection of the guard. Would you like to complete the inspection, SIR?"

Jep looked at the inspector in a way which let the inspector know that Jep was taking over. He walked down the line, bypassing Liam, Ezra, Jrasta and DOHNK. He came to the last guard in line and gave him a look which left the guard in tears. He wept harder and harder till the inspector came up and consoled the poor guard. From this moment on, the inspector looked at Jep with a newfound fear in his eyes.

Jep then signaled for Liam, Ezra and the others to follow him as they left the courtyard and made their way to the same doorway the inspector had used a few moments before. They found a stairway on the other side which took them up a level. At the top of the stairs was a large room. It was the guard's mess hall. A few guards were still finishing up their breakfast but rose to their feet when they saw Jep. He looked at them in such a way as to tell them, "As you were," and led the group out the far door.

Both Jep and Jrasta knew their way around the castle and led them directly to the throne room, although by a different route than they had come in before. As they approached the room, they stepped softly in the hopes of sneaking in undetected.

The door leading into the throne room was wide open, but the room itself was quiet. Liam looked and saw the throne empty and saw the chest off to the left side. A little beyond the chest were two large glass doors leading out to a balcony. On the right side of the room, a curtain had been put up to cut off a section of the room. This was different than the last time they had been in this room. Ezra, when he saw the chest, almost bolted for it right away, but Jrasta stopped him with a hand on his shoulder and signaled for him to be quiet.

They began to make their way across the room toward the chest as silently as possible. When they were halfway to their target, a deep, slow laugh reverberated through the room. They feared they had been caught. The laugh continued and grew even louder. No one dared move. The laugh was both sinister as well as somewhat contagious. Ezra started chuckling to himself and Liam soon followed. In no time, both Jrasta and DOHNK were laughing as well. All four tried to be as quiet as they could but found they could not stop laughing. Finally, Jep broke in with his chicken laughter. Unfortunately, he was anything but quiet. His laugh was almost as loud, if not louder, than the deep slow laugher.

With Jep's laughter echoing through the room, the deep laughter stopped. A voice was heard from the other side of the curtain, "Who's laughing? Who's out there?"

The curtain swung back to reveal the Regent and six guards. One of the guards stood there with a book called, "Guard Jokes: Funny Stories to Let Down Your Guard."

The Regent stared at them for a moment, trying to take in what he was seeing. Recognition dawned on him, and he screamed, "It's them! Arrest them!"

24. Revolution

Liam drew his sword and saw the others had done the same. Jep had both his little spears out and stood ready to fight as the guards ran toward them. Liam remembered how the other guards he had fought were strong, but slow, and readied himself. There were six guards, one for each of them and, of course, two for Jep.

The guards clearly intended just to crash into them, maybe bowling them over and overpowering them. Although the guards charging both Liam and Ezra were bigger than either boy, Jrasta had taught them well. They knew the key to fighting was not to resist the strength of the guard but to use his strength against him. Both Liam and Ezra simply stepped aside and stuck out their foot for the oncoming guard. Each of their opponents went sprawling, face first into the wall behind them.

Normal men would have been knocked unconscious when their heads hit the stone wall, but these guards had thick skulls. They stood up, shook their heads and turned ready to attack again. They advanced on Liam and Ezra, but this time wary of the two young men. Liam noticed the swords in the guard's hands were more like metal clubs than swords. They were sharp, but they were really thick. He knew if he simply tried to block a swing, the weight of the sword with the strength of the guard would seriously injure him.

As the guards stepped forward, Liam and Ezra moved fast, avoiding their opponent's swords and stepping around behind the men. Both boys had the exact same idea. It was one which would work well with an opponent as slow and dimwitted as these men. They ran their swords up the sides of the men, under their armor and sliced the ties holding their armor on. Two breastplates fell to the ground, and the guards looked down in horror as they realized they were exposed against opponents who were much faster than they and had very sharp swords.

Each guard swung their sword again. Liam deflected his opponent's sword over his head, using the momentum to spin the guard around and stick the sword up against the man's back. The man froze in place, knowing he was defeated.

Ezra was a little more daring. He simply stepped forward with his sword in hand as the guard's sword swung around him. Ezra eased his sword up against the guard's neck as the guard's sword continued to swing, coming around and putting Ezra in a hug. The guard felt the tip of Ezra's sword and dropped his own, holding up both hands and begging for mercy.

Jrasta and DOHNK seemed to be doing quite well with their guards. Jrasta had his guard down on his knees and calling out, "I surrender, I surrender!" DOHNK, on the other hand, was engaged in an all-out sword battle. It was clear she was just playing with the guard. She was highly skilled with the sword and could easily disarm him at any moment.

Jep was sitting down, picking at his wings with his beak. He seemed quite comfortable perched on top of a pile of two unconscious guards. He looked bored, as if the time it took to wait for the others to finish up with their guards was too much for him.

All three then turned their attention back to the Regent. His face had gone pale, and he appeared to be trying to say something. His jaw moved up and down, but no words came out.

Finally, he managed to find his voice. "How did you... my guards were..." He took a moment and composed himself. Straightening his large hat, he said in a very authoritative voice, "How dare you! You come in here and attack the Regent's guards! This is treason! I will have you arrested and locked away for the rest of your lives."

Jrasta spoke up, silencing the defeated ruler. "No, Ree-Gee. You are the traitor here. For centuries, our nation has been ruled by the one named in the chest. The key had been stolen and should have been retrieved years ago, but you just left it with Kenny the Dragon. Now that we have retrieved it, you should be the first one to want to open the chest as you are the one to lead our nation till the king comes, but you have betrayed us. The chest will now be opened, and the new king will decide what to do with you."

Jrasta grabbed the rope from the curtains and quickly tied up all the guards. Once the chest was open and the new king was named, none of them would dare to challenge the new ruler, but for now, they were willing to follow the Regent in his rebellion. Jrasta had some rope left and advanced on the Regent.

"Please, don't tie me up. I will not fight you. I have done what is wrong. I have rebelled against the laws of Arestana and disgraced myself among the people. Please, don't humiliate me any further."

Jrasta thought for a moment and agreed. He did not trust the Regent anymore but was willing to show this kindness to him. They moved over to the chest, grabbed the handles and started to drag it toward the balcony.

Liam and Ezra each had a handle. Neither boy thought the chest would be as heavy as it was. It was nearly impossible to lift. Instead, it scraped along the floor, leaving scratches behind them as they went.

DOHNK moved ahead and opened the balcony doors. As soon as the doors were opened, they could hear the sound of many voices. Liam wondered what was going on. Masha was supposed to gather the people outside, but there was not only the sound of a crowd but also of yelling and screaming.

Stepping out on the balcony, he looked down on the countless people below. They were yelling, screaming and throwing things at guards.

It appeared as though the entire city had gathered in the courtyard and streets below. The gates of the castle had been knocked down, and the people were pressing forward into the courtyard. The courtyard was filling with angry people, and many guards were trying to protect the castle from the group of disgruntled citizens.

In the center of the street, just outside the castle gates, a fountain rose above the people. It had a pool all around with a statue of some ancient king or hero or someone with a sword in hand. It was on a platform in the middle of the water. Hanging off the statue was a hairy creature yelling commands to people about how they should storm the castle. Apparently, after this was done, she would make them some soup.

Liam could see things were getting out of hand and feared if this wasn't stopped soon, people might get hurt or worse. Jrasta must have noticed the same thing as he ran to the edge of the balcony and hollered out, "Stop! Listen up! We have the key and the chest! Stop!!!"

No one listened. They kept pressing forward. Masha didn't seem to hear Jrasta either. Instead, she just kept inciting the people to move on toward the inner doors of the castle. Many in the crowd were carrying clubs or torches or large rocks. Things were about to get serious, but Liam realized they had no way to stop this. Each one looked at one another in fear. Liam wondered if they had done the right thing in getting Masha to gather the people together.

At that moment, something caught the attention of the people. The crowd quieted down and stopped pushing forward. The guards were no longer resisting the crowd; instead, they were standing at attention. Even Masha, hanging on the statue by her right arm, stopped yelling about soup and used her free hand to hold her eyebrows up so she could see better.

Liam looked to his left. Standing on the edge of the balcony was a majestic looking rooster. Jep was balanced on the railing with head held high and one wing stretched out over the people. Most looked at him in silence, although some could be heard saying, "Jep is about to speak. Listen up, everyone."

Jep then turned to Liam and looked at him with eyes that said, "Go ahead, Liam. They are ready to listen."

Liam looked out over the crowd. He felt a great deal of nervousness as the people looked on, waiting for him to tell them what was happening. He cleared his throat and swallowed hard. His mouth was dry.

"People of Kings-Home, hear me!" He thought that sounded like the kind of thing to say to this crowd. "I am a traveler from a world called Earth."

At that, people began mumbling among themselves. "Does he live underground? Is he a worm?" Jrasta waved at them and nodded a very confident, "Yes" back to the crowd.

Liam decided not to respond to this line of thought but instead pushed forward with his speech. "I have come here to complete a quest. My quest was to find the key to open the chest which will tell you who your new king is going to be. We have traveled a great distance and fought many creatures. We have…"

With that, a group of people started calling out, "Get to the point, Worm-Boy! We know who you are and what you were supposed to do. If you have the key, tell us and then open the chest!"

Liam realized he was being too formal and too wordy. "Umm… sorry, everyone. I have the key right here." He pulled the chain from around his neck and out from under his shirt. He held it high for all to see. When the crowd saw the key, they cheered and yelled, "Long live Traveler Worm-Boy. At least live long enough to open the chest, then we really don't care what happens to you! Long live Traveler Worm-Boy!"

Liam looked at the crowd with disappointment. He shook his head and stretched out his arm to hand the key to Jrasta.

Jrasta pushed his hand back saying, "No, Liam, this chest is for you to open. You may unlock it and see who the new king will be. Maybe it'll even be you!"

"But I don't want it to be me! I want to go home to be with my family!" Liam said, quite alarmed. He worried that if he was named king, there would be no way home for him.

"Open the chest, and we will see what we find," DOHNK said, putting her hand on his shoulder. "One thing at a time, Liam."

Liam knelt down before the chest. His hands were sweaty, and he worried he'd drop the key, but it slid smoothly into the lock. He turned the key and heard a soft click. The crowd was silent, waiting anxiously for the name of the new king to be read.

Liam lifted the lid and was surprised to see nothing inside, but a simple little piece of paper. He wasn't sure what he had expected but thought there might be something more elaborate. He picked up the note and found it was folded over, the name of the new king apparently written inside.

He thought about how nervous he felt before when trying to speak in front of everyone, but that was nothing compared to how he felt at this point. What was written on the inside of the piece of paper would determine the new king. The new king would set the direction for the country, for good or for ill, for years to come. But worse than all that, the new king could be him! He might never be able to leave Arestana and go home to his family.

His worried thinking was interrupted by a slap. Red ooze dripped down his face. Someone had thrown a rotten tomato at his face and hit him directly in the eye. The guy with the tomatoes was standing down in the crowd. He yelled up, "Get on with it, Worm-Boy! Stop thinking about opening up the note and open up the note! We want to know who our new king is!"

Liam made a mental note to find some reason to arrest that man if his name was on the inside of the piece of paper. If he were made king, this world would change some of its habits!

He opened up the note and read the name inside. His mouth dropped open as the implications of this message hit him. With a shaky voice, he read the words on the inside of the note, fearful that the crowd would hear the name and storm the castle out of anger and disappointment. "The new king of Arestana is... Jep the Chicken."

There was silence as everyone took in this information. All eyes turned toward Jep and Jep stared open-beaked at Liam. No one said anything till a lone voice rang out, "Long live King Jep!"

The whole crowd erupted in loud cheers. People jumped up and down and hugged each other. A new era in Arestana was about to begin. An era of Chicken-Rule.

25. Celebration

The celebrations began immediately. People set up tables in the streets and brought out food. The cooks in the castle's kitchens went to work, and the guards all made sure their armor was polished to a shiny perfection.

There was no real crowning ceremony needed as the note was all that was required for Jep to be recognized as king. Instead, the royal tailor came out and measured the chicken for some royal clothes, the royal carpenters came out and measured so they could build an appropriately sized throne to protect their new king from getting a royal pain in his butt and the royal goldsmith came out and measured in order to make a crown which would fit just perfectly.

Normally some of these items would simply need to be adjusted to fit the new king, but as this was their first chicken king, they needed to start from scratch with most of the royal items.

Jrasta ran in and untied the guards. Liam thought that might be a little unwise, but as Jrasta had explained, they were loyal to the crown. They would serve the Regent while he ruled, but as soon as the king was recognized, they would serve him completely. The only one they would need to deal with now was the Regent. Not that he would rebel, but his punishment would need to be determined by the new king. Liam looked around and saw that the former Regent had placed himself in a chair in the corner, waiting for King Jep's ruling.

As they all returned to the throne room, a crowd of singers came in and began to sing a rather off-tune song about the heroic accomplishments of King Jep the Mighty. The throne itself had already been removed from the room, and the carpenter had returned with a temporary throne for Jep to sit on. Jep walked to the steps leading to the throne and with difficulty, climbed up on the first step. He turned around to look at everyone, and each person in the room bowed to him, including the Regent.

Everyone had a happy look on their face and seemed quite content to be ruled by a chicken. The singers began to sing about the hope and future they had as a nation due to the wonder of their new king.

As Liam looked back at King Jep, he realized the people had grown quiet, and Jep himself was looking right at him. He looked at Liam in such a way as if to say, "Approach the throne, my child." Liam didn't like being called a child by a chicken but thought he should not challenge a king.

Liam came close and knelt before the king. The thought running through his head was, "How can a chicken rule a kingdom?" But as Liam looked deep into Jep's eyes, he began to see wisdom and a depth of understanding. He saw kindness and strength. He saw eyes that declared insight into all matters. Yes, Jep would be a good king.

Jep motioned for one of his personal guards to come forward. He brought a tiny little sword to his new king. Jep leaned

216

out and placed the tip on Liam's shoulders, knighting him "Sir Liam the Stinky."

Liam was grateful to be knighted and thought that was cool, but wasn't too pleased with a title of "Sir Liam the Stinky." He wasn't sure he wanted to be known by a name like that, nor did he think he was deserving of it. Aside from the times when he needed a shower. "Oh wait," thought Liam. "That was likely what it was about."

He was still tempted to ask for a different title when he noticed Jep look at Ezra. Ezra came over and knelt beside Liam as King Jep knighted him as well. Ezra was named, "Sir Ezra the Smelly." Liam looked at Ezra's face, and he saw his friend was absolutely beaming with pride. Clearly, this was a very positive thing here.

"Thank you, King Jep," Ezra said, bowing his head to the Chicken King. Liam realized he had been rude and quickly thanked King Jep as well.

Jep turned to Liam and gave him a look which Liam couldn't quite figure out. He stared into Liam's eyes as Liam knelt there, wondering what he was supposed to do. Jep leaned in, and Liam wondered if the knighting process was incomplete. Jep's mouth opened, and Liam realized too late what was about to happen.

Jep clamped down on his nose and held on for dear life. Liam was about to scream and try to yank the chicken off but remembered that Jep was now King of Arestana and he should probably show a great deal of respect for him. Besides, he wondered from the way Jep was hanging on if his nose would come off in Jep's beak. He continued kneeling in the same spot feeling his eyes tear up while Jep continued to clamp down on his nose. It was a painful experience, and he was not overly pleased with it. Certainly not in front of everyone.

After what seemed like an hour, Jep finally let go. When Liam stood up and looked around, he noticed a lineup had formed behind him, with Ezra next in line. Ezra knelt down, and Jep latched on, followed by DOHNK, Jrasta, the Regent, about twenty guards, the stable boy, some chickens and finally Masha. Liam couldn't help but notice King Jep didn't bite down quite as hard or hold as long on other people as he had on Liam's nose.

The celebration lasted well into the evening, with multiple nose bites along the way. It seemed to be Jep's thing and was quickly becoming a kingdom-wide practice. Everywhere Liam went, he would see people biting one another's noses, and he could see teeth marks where others had had someone clamp down. As he moved among the people, he was often greeted as Sir Liam, and he could hear people whisper about him behind his back, with awe and respect calling him, "Sir Liam the Stinky."

He hung out with Ezra as the day went on, occasionally bumping into Jrasta or DOHNK. There were jugglers and street performers. There were singers and magicians. There were acrobats and fire-eaters. People were dancing in the street and children were running around playing. There was plenty of food everywhere they went. The city was one big party.

At just after supper time, Liam felt something. He felt it and he kind of heard it. It was like a voice calling to him, but he couldn't make out the words. It was like a pull on his chest, but he could see no string or rope attached.

He knew what was going on. The pull had begun, and it was time for him to return to his home. He hoped it didn't lead to a toilet again.

He was so excited about going home. He missed his parents so much and knew they must be worried sick. He had been gone for around two weeks, as best as he could figure. He wondered if they had given up on him being alive. Maybe they simply thought he was dead and they had moved on. Maybe they had emptied his room and turned it into a small bakery. He knew that was silly. They would wait at least three weeks before engaging in such a huge renovation.

But as excited as he was about returning to his home, he was also going to miss Arestana. Not the world so much, but he would miss Ezra, Jrasta, DOHNK and Jep. He even thought he might miss Masha, although he doubted it.

"What's wrong?" Ezra was staring at Liam with a concerned look on his face.

"I'm feeling the pull. It's what I felt just as I was being drawn into this world. It's time for me to go back home."

Ezra looked at Liam, clearly upset. They had grown quite close over the last little while. "I don't want you to go home. Why don't you just stay here! You can stay with me. We can keep going on adventures. Maybe we can live in the castle since we're Knights and we're friends with the king."

Part of Liam wanted to stay, but he knew this wasn't his home and his heart longed to be back with his parents. "Thanks, Ezra, but I have to go home. I want to go home. I miss my family."

Ezra looked quite sad but nodded his head. He understood.

"I just don't how to get back. I think I feel the pull to head that way down the street." Liam pointed in a direction away from the castle.

"Well, let's go. We'll find your way back together." Ezra was a good friend.

They started to walk down the street, and as people recognized them, they would greet them saying, "Hello, Sir Liam and Sir Ezra!" The boys waved back and kept going. Some people asked where they were going. When Liam told them it was time for him to go back to his world, they joined in with him to see him off.

He started to recognize some in the crowd from the Booger Village. He noticed Jrasta and DOHNK, as well as Masha, join in. It was good to have his friends with him as he set out to return to his home.

They came to a corner, and Liam felt the tug pulling him down a side-street. As he turned the corner, the crowd parted for him. He looked at their faces and saw respect, mixed with sorrow for his leaving. They were his friends, and he knew he'd always be welcome back in Arestana.

He looked up ahead to see what lay before him and what he saw caused him to cry out. In a loud, frustrated voice he yelled, "Oh you've got to be kidding me!"

There before him, at the end of the crowd, at the end of the side-street was his destination. It was an outhouse. He had hoped he would never have to take that route again.

Ezra looked at him with pity in his eyes. "I had heard that travelers usually have to return home the same way they came to Arestana. I didn't know you came through something like that. I hope it's not as bad as it looks."

Ezra and Liam hugged, followed by Jrasta and then DOHNK. Some stranger came up and gave him an uncomfortably long hug as well which required Jrasta and DOHNK's help to pull the person off him.

He then turned to the outhouse. Everyone began to clap as he walked the pathway created by the crowd toward his "doorway" home. As he drew near, he smelled a horrific smell. Opening the door, he saw a small, dark room with a bench in it. The bench had two holes in it, obviously set up so two people could share. He was grateful no one was currently using one of the holes. He turned around and waved goodbye to his friends as they returned their good-byes and told him they hoped he could come back someday.

Liam closed the door, and the crowd outside seemed to get quiet. He looked down at the holes in the seat of the outhouse and wondered what would happen next. When this happened at home, he didn't have to wait; it just sucked him in. He looked down and saw some terrible things in the bottom of the outhouse, but it didn't look like the swirling colors of the portal which, he assumed, would take him home.

Nothing seemed to be going on at first, but then the tug came stronger. He looked again into the holes in the bench and this time saw the familiar swirl of colors and felt the wind pick up. The wind, unfortunately, didn't help at all with the smell. It just seemed to make it worse. It also seemed to splash something wet around the tiny enclosure.

He had a moment of doubt. He wasn't sure going home was worth being sucked through an outhouse. He turned to grab the handle and braced his feet so they wouldn't be sucked in as they had been last time. He resisted for a moment or two but then lost his footing. This time, however, he didn't go in feet first. He went in butt first. In fact, his butt got stuck in the hole in the bench, and he felt like he had just clogged a giant vacuum. The sound grew loud, and he hollered out for help.

The door swung open. As he looked out over the crowd, he realized he didn't want anyone to see him this way as he was now sucked in up to his knees and shoulders. Only his head, arms and from the knees down were still visible to the crowd. The rest was down the hole.

All his friends looked on in horror at his shoulders and feet sticking out of the hole. He managed to say, "This didn't go as planned," before his body slipped in the rest of the way and he was no more in Arestana.

26. Harry

It wasn't hard to settle back in at home. It was difficult, of course, to explain to his parents why he had been missing for two weeks. The police took statement after statement, and no one quite believed him. He didn't blame them. It was an odd story, for sure. At first, he was tempted to make up some lie, but he believed lying was wrong and there was also something fun about the idea of telling people all the details of Arestana.

His parents comforted him in the way they knew best. They baked him many desserts and tried to listen to the stories of his experiences. Most of the time they just shook their heads, but after a while, Liam began to wonder if they were starting to believe him. He hoped one day they truly could.

School returned to normal. He wasn't a big fan of school, but it was nice to have a normal life again. The big thing that changed, though, was the whole situation with Harry.

Two days after he had returned to the real world, Liam met up with Harry. He was walking home and turned a corner. As he turned, he expected to see what one would normally expect to see around a corner—a new street with a new sidewalk—but instead ran into a large Harry shaped wall.

"Hello, Ed," Harry said, looking mean and ready to teach Liam a lesson for being away for so long.

"Hello, Harry. What a wonderful day for a walk!" Liam said. He realized he was about to try to provoke Harry and thought that might be a foolish move, but if he could take on a giant sea monster, certainly he could stand up to Harry. "You're looking mighty slow today. Are you wearing a new shirt?"

Harry looked confused, or perhaps more confused than usual. "No, I don't think my shirt is slow… or new… or… what was the question?"

"I think you should step out of my way and let me go home," Liam replied. He had faced soldiers, a dragon, giant Kittens and a Kraken. He no longer found Harry to be much of a threat.

"I think I should pound you into jelly. Then I should make a sandwich. A peanut butter and honey sandwich." Harry replied.

Liam thought this through for a moment and wondered if he should point out any one of the many problems with Harry's idea. He then realized he would have to work hard to help Harry understand what he had missed. He decided to miss the point himself instead. "Sounds tasty. Can I have half of the sandwich?"

"No, you are going to be the sandwich!" Harry replied, although there was a look of uncertainty in his eyes.

"Tell you what. How about I make the sandwich, and then both of us can have some!" Liam thought a little peacemaking would take away some of the hostility in Harry's eyes and maybe even add some more confusion.

"Well, I am hungry, but then I won't get to pound you into the ground!" Harry explained, a little less sure of himself.

"I thought you wanted to pound me into jelly. If you pound me into the ground, you won't have any jelly and then how are you going to make your peanut butter and honey sandwich?" This was starting to be a lot of fun.

"What? I don't... hey... ahhh... alright, you asked for it. Here comes the pain!" Harry pulled back his right arm and got ready to bring on the "pain."

Liam stood ready. He had had enough practice with hand to hand combat over the last while to not be too concerned about Harry. He was like a non-dangerous guard. Strong, but slow. Harry just didn't have a sword or any armor.

As the swing came toward him, Liam simply pushed it aside and waited for another. The second swing came from the left and Liam did the same again. Harry looked at Liam with a lot of anger and jumped right at him. Liam calmly stepped out of the way and gave a little push to help speed Harry along on his way to the sidewalk. Harry hit the sidewalk hard.

Liam walked over to him and rolled him over. He looked down at poor Harry. The confusion was growing by the second. No one had ever stood up to Harry before, and he wasn't sure what to do about it. Liam bent down and found himself drawn to finish him off. Not in a violent way, but to put an end to the bullying once and for all. At first, he thought it was a bad idea, but he found he couldn't resist. He leaned in close to Harry and stretched out his teeth. He chomped down on Harry's nose.

Liam held on. Their eyes met, and the look in Harry's eyes was one of shock. Neither boy moved for a moment. Harry looked like he couldn't make sense of why someone would be biting his nose. Liam didn't find this to be a surprise. He himself tried to make sense of why he was biting Harry's nose. They looked at each other again, and Liam realized this might work for Jep, but it was a bad idea for Liam. Liam released, and Harry got to his feet. Harry stared at Liam with a mixture of unbelief and horror in his eyes.

Liam stood up and took a step back. He felt very awkward.

"Ed?"

"Yes, Harry?"

"Did you just bite my nose?" Harry wiped some saliva from his face.

"I think I did," Liam replied.   He felt embarrassed and disgusted.

"I think I'll leave you alone for now. Let's just not be around each other anymore, Ed."

"That sounds good," Liam replied.

The two boys parted ways. Neither spoke of the nose bite again for a long time.

For Liam, the next two months were pretty normal. At least till Liam once again felt the pull.

Chapter One from Arestana II
The Defense Quest
Coming June 4, 2018

Book II: The Zoo

"Silence!" screamed Mrs. Horgenborden. Liam's eighth grade teacher did not approve of happiness, and some of the students on the bus had made the mistake of smiling.

They were heading to the zoo, and Liam wished he could be just about anywhere else. The zoo was fun, but not on a school trip. He didn't want to take a tour, and he didn't want to deal with all the other kids.

The other students were hard to get along with. Some of them avoided him, some picked on him, and some just ignored him. He had never really fit in with the other kids.

What made it worse was that about two months before, he had been flushed down a toilet into another world. The flushing part wasn't his favorite, but he had liked the other world.

While in this other world, he had learned to fight with a sword and ride a war horse. He had battled a dragon and fought off a horde of skeletons. He had also met some pretty great friends there. Liam and his friends had been given a quest while in that world, and it had taken him about two weeks to complete it. When he was done, he was flushed back home.

It had been an adventure of a lifetime, but it didn't help him with his friend situation at home. He had been gone to this world for about two weeks. The world was named Arestana, and it was the strangest place Liam could ever imagine. It was strange, but he had grown to love it.

When he had arrived home, he found out some people just thought he had run away and then come back when he had had enough of living on the streets. Some thought he had been kidnapped. One of the kids actually suspected Liam was part of a spy ring and had gone on a mission. Liam encouraged that idea. Most people now just looked at him as though he was a little more odd than they had once thought.

The one relationship he hadn't expected to change much was with Harry. Harry was a rather large bully. He had picked on Liam for years and seemed to be quite creative in his ability to mess up Liam's day.

When Liam had arrived back home, Harry apparently felt it was his job to punish Liam for being away. He hadn't realized, however, that Liam was no longer the same kid he had been before. Harry was upset at not being able to pick on Liam for a couple weeks and had expected to teach Liam a lesson for ruining his bullying schedule. Liam had simply knocked Harry down and bit his nose. That last part was something Liam had wanted to forget, and it was not something he was about to talk to Harry about. Harry also seemed willing to avoid speaking of it, so Liam never brought it up.

Harry had avoided Liam for a little while after his return to this world—and after the nose biting incident—but in time he had started to hang around Liam. Harry had never had anyone stand up to him before, and it seemed like Harry was happy to find someone he couldn't bully.

The last few weeks had been weird. Harry now seemed to think of Liam as a friend. He hung out with Liam on the weekends and followed him everywhere. Liam was shocked to find that Harry was actually kind of fun to be around.

Someone large sat down next to Liam on the bus. He smelled Harry's familiar scent. Harry normally smelled like onions, garlic or stolen lunch money. Oddly enough, stolen lunch money in large enough quantities actually had a scent. Today, Harry's smell was garlic. Harry was also wearing his "Zoo Hat." It was actually just a regular Chicago Bears cap, but Harry insisted it was the hat he always wore to the zoo.

"Hello, Ed." Harry had never quite caught on to the fact that Liam's name wasn't "Ed." He called Liam "Ed" all the time, and Liam had learned to just roll with it.

"Hey, Harry. Nice hat."

"Thanks. I can't wait to see the monkeys. They're my favorite. I like the ones with horns." Harry had a big smile on his face.

Liam thought the "horn" comment was odd but no more odd than anything else he and Harry talked about.

"When we get there, I'm going to buy you a monkey treat. They taste really good. They're spicy. They're hotter than fire," Harry said with a big smile on his face.

"You find yourself eating a lot of fire, Harry?" Liam wasn't paying an awful lot of attention to the conversation. He had developed the ability to chat with someone without actually giving much thought to what the person was saying. This ability had gotten him in trouble a few times before, but for the most part, it was a handy skill.

His mind drifted to Arestana again. He wondered what his friends were up to. Ezra was likely getting in trouble with the guards at the castle. DOHNK was likely practicing her awesome sword skills. Masha was likely feeding some poor soul her soup in her special, violent way.

The bus jolted to a stop and Liam came back to reality. They had arrived at the zoo.

Mrs. Horgenborden stood up at the front and glared at everyone till they quieted down. Mrs. Horgenborden was somewhat like a lemon... sour. The bus driver sneezed unexpectedly, and Mrs. Horgenborden looked like she was about to drag him off the bus and teach him a lesson. He began to weep and apologized to her. Between tears, he mumbled something about failing at everything he had ever put his mind to. Mrs. Horgenborden looked pleased and turned back to the class.

"Listen up, little children!" Mrs. Horgenborden yelled at her class. She seemed convinced every student she taught was about four years old.

"We're here at the zoo for you to learn stuff! Information!" she yelled. "You are NOT here to enjoy yourself. Learning is not supposed to be fun and will not be fun as long as I live on this wretched earth. We will be here for the entire afternoon, and I have arranged a tour guide to lead us through the zoo. If I catch any of you smiling or looking like you are enjoying yourself, I'll personally feed you to the lions."

Liam wasn't sure Mrs. Horgenborden had actually said any of that, but he sometimes found his imagination running wild when she spoke. Life was a lot more boring after his time in Arestana.

Liam continued daydreaming. When he thought Mrs. Horgenborden had finished speaking, he stood up. Everyone gasped and looked at him as if he had done something unforgivable. He sat down immediately before Mrs. Horgenborden could reach for his throat.

His teacher glared at him before continuing. "As I was saying, does anyone think this is going to be fun today? If so, come up here, and I'll teach you a lesson." Liam was pretty sure she hadn't said that either, but his attitude toward school and Mrs. Horgenborden hadn't been the best lately.

When the teacher had finished her lecture, everyone grabbed their bags as they made their way to the door. Harry pulled Liam to his feet and started to drag him to the front, pushing their classmates to the side as he went.

Liam could see Mrs. Horgenborden watch Harry pull Liam past all the kids. She seemed to be faced with a bit of a problem. She did not approve of enthusiasm or excitement, nor did she approve of kids pushing other kids out of the way, but she did approve of Harry. She seemed to have a soft spot for large, mean kids smelling of onions or garlic. She let him pass with a kind smile but glared at Liam as Harry dragged him off the bus.

Harry seemed beside himself with excitement. The zoo was perhaps his favorite place on earth. It wasn't the lions or the monkeys or the giraffes. It wasn't any of the actual animals. It was the habitats that caught his eye. He just loved seeing how everything from the small cages to the large open areas were put together. He would watch closely to see how food went in or out, running to various habitats at feeding time just to see the workers dump food through holes or open doors to feed the animals. He couldn't care less about the actual animals; he just wanted to see how they lived.

They came up to the gate. Mrs. Horgenborden yelled at the gatekeeper for a few minutes, and they entered into the zoo. It really was a pretty amazing zoo. The signs and pictures and walkways alone were enough to grab your attention, but the collection of animals was enough to keep you fascinated for hours!

Mrs. Horgenborden entered into a small room labeled, "Office" and emerged a few minutes later, followed by a tour guide in tears. The guide came and stood before Liam's class.

"Little children! Pay attention! This man is going to be our tour guide. He doesn't know much, so be patient with him." Mrs. Horgenborden crossed her arms and glared at the poor man as if to ask, "Is there something I said that you didn't like?"

The man looked back, apologized to her for living and turned to the students. "My name is... Caaahhgghh!" Everyone froze in terror. They weren't sure what Mrs. Horgenborden would do to the tour guide for coughing mid-introduction. For that matter, they weren't sure what she would do to them because he coughed.

"I'm sorry, my name is Brian. I will be your tour guide this afternoon. Welcome to the Eastside Zoo. We will be taking what is called the Savanah tour first where we will..."

Liam noticed someone had invaded his personal space. He could tell because there was a warm garlic aroma and the feel of someone's breath on his cheek. He turned to see Harry's face only inches from his own. Liam pulled back quickly.

"Let's go!" Harry said in a creepy, airy sort of way. "This may be our only chance." Harry had a tendency to drool a bit when he was excited.

"Our only chance to do what?" Liam looked at Harry with confusion.

"Our chance to get out of here and do our own tour of the place!"

Liam was about to suggest that they wait till after the field trip and after school to break from the rest of the students, when Harry grabbed his arm and started to drag him down a path which read, "Aqua-World."

"Let's take a look at the aquariums first. I hear the glass is ten feet thick!"

Liam wasn't sure that was true, but he didn't know it was wrong either. While in Arestana he had learned to just roll with a lot of things, so Liam didn't get too worked up with what his friend said. Harry could have said the glass was a mile thick and Liam would have just carried on.

231

They explored through all the aquariums. Liam enjoyed the fish and the whales. The shark tank was awesome, and even the massive goldfish were pretty cool.

They explored the zoo, one habitat at a time. Liam looked at the animals while Harry checked out the walls and glass and fences of the various cages. They moved through each of the displays at a pretty good speed and managed to get through most of the afternoon without even seeing the rest of the class.

Near the end of the day, there was one close call where they came around the corner and nearly walked right into Mrs. Horgenborden as she was yelling at a random parent pushing a stroller. Liam thought he heard something about it not being the right way to push a child through a zoo. Harry wasn't the fastest kid in some ways, but he was quick when he needed to be. He grabbed Liam and yanked him behind a kiosk selling snacks before they could be seen.

"They'll never catch us! I'll protect you, Ed! If they see us, make a run for the lion cage. They'll never follow us in there," Harry said with wild eyes.

Liam thought things were escalating quickly and wasn't sure he wanted to be a part of what Harry had in mind. At the same time, this was the closest he'd come to any form of adventure in what seemed like an eternity. He decided to just roll with this as he did with most things.

When the tour guide had led the class and Mrs. Horgenborden on to the next stop, Harry pulled Liam out from behind the kiosk and led him in the opposite direction. "There's something I want to show you, Ed. It's the most amazing thing you've ever seen. I guarantee it!"

They ran down a pathway which Liam strongly suspected was one of those, "Employees Only" type of deals and came to an area of the zoo which appeared to be under construction. There were no animals as far as he could see in any of the habitats and each of them were at varying levels of development. There were some which looked nearly ready for their animals and others which just had a hole dug in the ground. One of the areas was just an open area of grass and weeds with nothing more than a single stake in the ground. Liam figured it was there to mark where a habitat or cage would one day be placed.

Harry led Liam through the maze of equipment and unfinished habitats till he found what he was looking for. It was an area surrounded by a wall which came up to about Liam's waist.

As they approached the side of that particular habitat, Liam looked down into the pit. There was a small area of water with a muddy area of ground next to it. Growing in the center were some trees and among the trees were some fake looking rocks.

Liam could tell Harry was quite excited but wasn't sure what it was that might cause him to reach this level of excitement. He looked over at his friend to find him nearly shaking with joy.

"I think we should do it," Harry said, gripping the wall with his hands while staring into the cage.

"Do what?" Liam thought this was odd even for Harry. Not Arestana level odd, for sure, but odd for Harry.

"I think we should go down inside the habitat and live here."

Liam looked at Harry for a moment. He was pretty sure he couldn't have heard Harry suggest they live at the zoo in this cage. He knew Harry loved the habitats at the zoo, but could he really love it so much that he felt living in one would be an okay option?

He looked down into the cage and was about to say, "Maybe some other time, Harry. I'd like to get back to the group," when Harry cheered.

Harry only heard the word, "maybe." To Harry, the word, "maybe" was a strong "Yes!"

Liam felt his feet leave the ground and was shocked to find how strong Harry was. Before Liam fully knew what was going on, he was falling through the air into the cage. As he plummeted to his death, he looked up in time to see Harry leap over the wall after him.

Continued in Arestana Book II: The Defense Quest
Coming June 4, 2018

*   *   *

If you like the Arestana Series, consider leaving reviews for this book on Amazon, Goodreads, Chapters and more! These reviews help more than you might realize… and they make Shawn feel good.

Pronunciation Guide

Note: the following pronunciation helps do not use official symbols or styles for proper pronunciation. This is partly because I (as the author) do not understand those symbols myself and partly due to the fact that it seems like a lot of work to figure them out. Soooo... the following is my own version of a pronunciation guide. The capital letters are where the emphasis is supposed to be. The lowercase letters... are not.

Achtor	ACK-tor
Arestana	air-eh-STAN-ah
Arestanian	air-eh-STAIN-ee-an
Aron	AIR-rawn
DOHNK	DOHNK!
Ezra	EZZ-ra
Jep	JEP
Jrasta	jer-AS-ta
Shawn	AWE-some
Toilet	TOY-let

Check out these books by Shawn P. B. Robinson

Jerry the Squirrel: Volume One

Arestana: The Key Quest

Arestana: The Defense Quest (Coming June 2018)

Arestana: The Harry Quest (Coming November 2018)

Join Liam on an exciting adventure as his normal day of school and bullies takes an unfortunate turn as he gets sucked down a toilet.

Yah… that's the kind of books we're talking about!

#bewarethechicken

Made in the USA
Columbia, SC
22 March 2018